Praise for
Woodson Falls: 2 Sunrise Trail

The Surprising Life of a Not-So-Sleepy Town Called Woodson Falls

Within the small town of Woodson Falls, neighbors and friends look out for each other. But then there is a fiery explosion and death at 2 Sunrise Trail. Uncovering the cause also exposes the complex relationship between real estate development, conservation and private goals in an exurban area. The main characters each are uniquely drawn with personalities that fit their roles in the town, including those who are active with the local land trust.

—Margery Josephson, PhD, former Board President of the Naromi Land Trust, Sherman, CT

Andrea O'Connor sets a new challenge for her sleuthing lawyer when a cherished client dies under questionable circumstances. A brisk read that further enriches the character of Gabriella Quinn, Esq., and her search for solace after devastating loss. *Woodson Falls: 2 Sunrise Trail* is a meditation on death, guilt and renewal. A rewarding read!

—Joseph Keneally, loyal reader

Andrea O'Connor's third Gaby Quinn mystery continues to provide a warm and cozy feel that has become the hallmark of this series. *Woodson Falls: 2 Sunrise Trail* brings small town politics front and center as trouble is brewing in the local land trust that spills out into the community. And when the land trust's beloved former director dies in a sudden explosion, Gaby must determine whether her client's death is accidental or intentional. A fine writing style moves the puzzle along at an effortless pace and Ms. O'Connor's lead character, Gaby Quinn, is a pleasure to follow around. *2 Sunrise Trail* is a good read for anyone who likes a clever mystery.

—Peter Green, author of the Jimmy Dugan mystery series

Andrea O'Connor delivers another twisting, winding legal thriller. In *Woodson Falls: 2 Sunrise Trail*, savvy and intelligent Attorney Gaby Quinn and Officer Matt Thomas truly become the romantic dynamic duo as they collaborate to unravel the town's latest mystery. With likable characters and dialogue that moves the story forward at every turn, O'Connor's latest puzzler is not just entertainment for mystery lovers but an education in the law. And human nature.

—Amy Nicholson, freelance writer

The Gaby Quinn Mystery series, written by Andrea O'Connor, is now on the third book in the series, *Woodson Falls: 2 Sunrise Trail*. Attorney Gaby Quinn's next case is for a very close friend, Winston Pinkham. He needed her help with a financial problem and didn't know what to do. Gaby was willing to help him. But… things happened unexpectedly. While he was home, there was an explosion in his house. Gaby now must become like a detective to find out what happened. Was it an accident or murder? There are so many twists and turns in this mystery. You get to know many of the residents in Woodson Falls along the way.

—Linda Kopec, author of *Cancer Gifts*

Woodson Falls: 2 Sunrise Trail is the third book in the Gaby Quinn Mystery series and the third that I've read. These mysteries are told from the point of view of a lawyer rather than the usual police detective. Gaby experienced a trauma in her past that resulted in her presence in the small and pretty town of Woodson Falls. Each of the books centers on the address of a person for whom Gaby is performing a legal service. This story has a financial angle as well as the unexpected death of a much-loved elderly client. Was it an accident? Or was he just careless? If not, who would want to harm this elderly, ill gentleman and why? Alongside the story of the client and his affairs are the development of the mystery of what happened to Gaby's husband and her growing relationship with Matt, the local state trooper, which adds extra interest both to her and her private life.

As always, the plot and character development are spot on and, after three visits to Woodson Falls, I am well invested in the area and its inhabitants! The ending to the story is satisfying, and we are left with a cliffhanger in the form of a new clue that may point to information about the past. What will it lead to? I look forward to finding out.

—Barbara Crompton, NetGalley reviewer

Woodson Falls:
2 Sunrise Trail

A Gaby Quinn Mystery

Woodson Falls:
2 Sunrise Trail

A Gaby Quinn Mystery

by

Andrea O'Connor

EMERALD LAKE
BOOKS
Sherman, Connecticut

Woodson Falls: 2 Sunrise Trail
Copyright © 2022 Andrea O'Connor
Cover design and illustration © 2022 by Mark Gerber

Books published by Emerald Lake Books may be ordered through your favorite booksellers or by visiting emeraldlakebooks.com.

Library of Congress Cataloging-in-Publication Data
Names: O'Connor, Andrea B., author.
Title: Woodson falls: 2 sunrise trail / by Andrea O'Connor.
Description: Sherman, Connecticut : Emerald Lake Books, [2022] | Series: A Gaby Quinn mystery ; 3 | Summary: "Attorney Gaby Quinn's law practice has continued to keep her busy, as has her budding relationship with Officer Matt Thomas. But she always has time to help a friend in need. So, when her elderly friend Winston Pinkham admits to being in a bit of a bind, she's quick to offer her assistance. But someone else has other plans..."-- Provided by publisher.
Identifiers: LCCN 2022036206 (print) | LCCN 2022036207 (ebook) | ISBN 9781945847684 (trade paperback) | ISBN 9781945847691 (epub)
Subjects: LCGFT: Novels.
Classification: LCC PS3615.C5843 W667 2022 (print) | LCC PS3615.C5843 (ebook) | DDC 813/.6--dc23/eng/20220812
LC record available at https://lccn.loc.gov/2022036206
LC ebook record available at https://lccn.loc.gov/2022036207

For Barrie Sachs, my dear friend and my very own Nell Whitney.
And always John, for all you've given me.

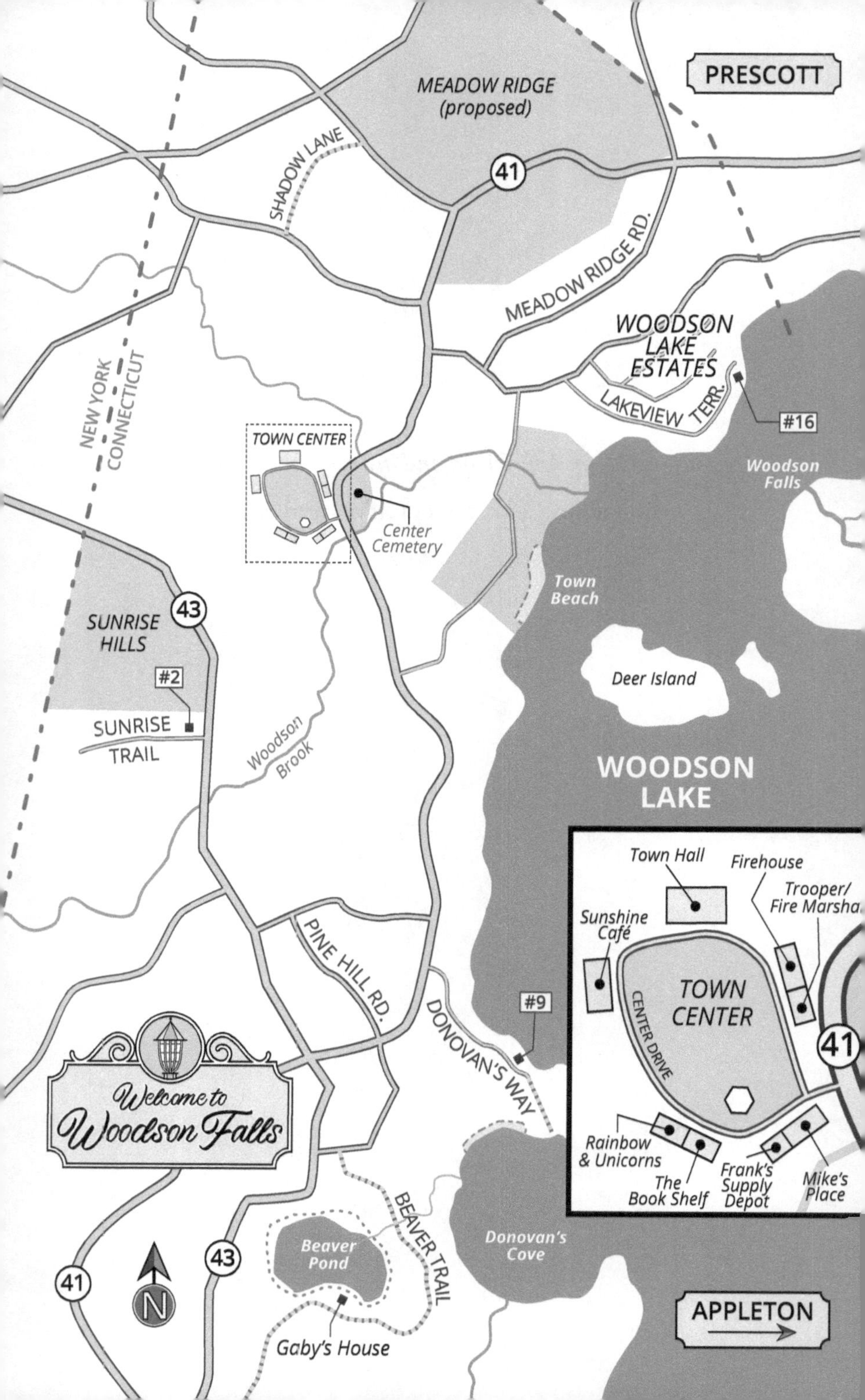

PRESCOTT
MEADOW RIDGE
(proposed)
41
SHADOW LANE
MEADOW RIDGE RD.
WOODSON LAKE ESTATES
LAKEVIEW TERR.
#16
NEW YORK
CONNECTICUT
TOWN CENTER
Center Cemetery
Woodson Falls
Town Beach
43
SUNRISE HILLS
#2
SUNRISE TRAIL
Woodson Brook
Deer Island
WOODSON LAKE
PINE HILL RD.
DONOVAN'S WAY
#9
Welcome to
Woodson Falls
Town Hall
Firehouse
Trooper/
Fire Marshal
Sunshine Café
TOWN CENTER
CENTER DRIVE
41
Rainbow
& Unicorns
The Book Shelf
Frank's Supply Depot
Mike's Place
BEAVER TRAIL
Beaver Pond
Donovan's Cove
41
N
43
Gaby's House
APPLETON

Prologue

"Philosophy Department, Marge Devereau speaking."

"Marge! Hello! Joe Quinn calling. I've been trying to reach Gaby, but she's not picking up her line."

"Hi, Joe! Sorry, Gaby's been tied up in oral defenses since ten this morning. Not even sure if she took time for lunch. These graduate students always put things off to the last minute, then expect the professors to drop everything so they can clear the last hurdle to their PhD's. But you know how Gaby is. She bends over backward to support her students."

"It's one of the many things I love about her. Her commitment to her work and to anything else she values—even me."

"Ha! Especially you, as if you don't already know that."

"Oh, I do. I'm a lucky man."

"Do you want me to go searching for her?"

"No, no. Just give her a message if you would."

"Of course!"

"Ask her to call me at work when she's done for the day, then meet me in front of my office building. I've got a surprise for her."

"What is it? Not her birthday, I know."

"No, nothing like that. I'll let her tell you tomorrow."

"Okay, Joe. Done. I won't leave here until I'm sure she's gotten the message."

"Great, and thanks. Have a lovely evening, Marge."

Joe was waiting for Gaby when she arrived at his office building on Madison Avenue. It was close to six, and the street was filled with people walking to the subway to go home, to the parking garage to retrieve their car, to Grand Central to catch their train, or just to their apartment at the end of a long workday.

Gaby hugged her husband of eight years, giving him a peck on the cheek. "What's up, hon? When Marge gave me the message to meet you at the office, she said you had a surprise?"

"Indeed I do, and I've made reservations for us at Risotto's to tell you all about it," Joe responded, putting his arm around his wife and directing her down the street.

"Our favorite place! What's the occasion, Joe?" she asked, grinning at his boyish excitement. "Must be happy news."

"It is! But first, how did work go today? Marge said you were tied up for most of it making new docs?" Joe looked down at his wife as they strolled along Madison Avenue.

"We got three doctoral candidates over the finish line—or at least they'll be done after they've made some minor editorial changes to their dissertations. Nothing too difficult, unlike the unfortunate few who have to be sent back to square one."

"You're too sweet to do that to a poor, starving student," Joe said with a chuckle, giving Gaby's shoulder a gentle squeeze.

"I hate it when we have to give a candidate that message, but sometimes academic integrity demands it, especially when it's a Columbia University degree that's being awarded," Gaby said, shaking her head.

They turned the corner onto a side street. "Here we are," Joe announced, opening the door to the small restaurant and pulling her in.

The maître d' greeted them at the door. "Welcome back to Risotto's. And how are the lovebirds this fine evening?"

"We're just great, Lorenzo," Joe said. "I called earlier to reserve our booth."

"Indeed," he responded, leading them to their usual table and offering them menus. "Will you be starting with a beverage? The usual?"

"Tonight, it's champagne for my lady and me," Joe answered. "We're celebrating."

"And may I ask what is the special occasion?"

"A big success," said Joe.

"And what would you prefer?"

"A Taittinger rosé, if you have it."

Nodding his head, Lorenzo announced, "I'm sure we do. Francesco will be your waiter this evening. I'll be right back with your champagne," Lorenzo said with a nod and a small smile as Joe reached across the table to grab Gaby's hand.

"I love you, Gaby," he murmured.

"Love you too, Joe," she answered, squeezing his hand. "With all my heart."

After their waiter had come by to fill their water glasses and place a basket of focaccia and a shallow dish of olive oil on the table, announcing the specials as he did so, Lorenzo returned with the champagne, two flutes and an ice bucket. Twisting the cork, which gave a satisfying "pop," he poured the bubbly drink into their glasses. "Enjoy!"

Joe winked at Gaby as he lifted his glass toward hers.

"Now, will you tell me what we're celebrating?" Gaby asked, toasting him with a clink of their glasses. The champagne was perfectly chilled and delectable.

"The people at Birch Products loved our presentation, Gaby! Especially the social media tie-in we were able to develop. Lots of ad firms are having trouble with that piece, and we nailed it. It's a big account. Really a coup for the firm."

"And for you!" she exclaimed. "I know you've been working hard on this one."

She grinned, sipping the champagne while listening to her husband's enthusiastic description of the creative advertising campaign the team he headed up had just completed for their newest client.

"We tried something new with this marketing project. I had a hunch my idea might be suited to their line of cleaning products. We had run several focus group sessions with people from their target audience. They were intrigued and enthusiastic. Always a good sign, but you never know how the client will react. Especially since this was a totally novel approach. I don't want to bore you with the details, just to bask in the glory of your praise and admiration." Joe grinned back at her, lifting his glass in a salute to them both.

"I'm thrilled for you, Joe. You're just so brilliant!" she said with a grin. "Guess we both did good today."

They ended up with a dessert for two following dinner to celebrate their achievements, then began walking home to their apartment. Gaby smiled to herself, treasuring her sense of comfort and security as they strolled arm-in-arm. They paused to kiss under a street lamp, absorbed in one another.

"Where am I?" Gaby asked the man seated at the head of the narrow cot she was lying on. The cot swayed as she became aware of being in a moving vehicle—the roar of traffic around them, the sound of a siren in the distance, the feel of the road rumbling beneath them.

"Where's Joe?" she asked, struggling to sit up, suddenly aware of a sharp pain in her right ankle, aches all over her body.

"Ma'am, you're in an ambulance on the way to Bellevue. Best if you lie still until we reach the hospital. You and the gentleman you were with were in a… an accident. Your foot was injured and…"

"What happened? Where's Joe?" Gaby interrupted the man, her voice rising in panic, making it difficult for her to breathe. She lifted her hand to her face, feeling something bulky and foreign covering the side of her face from her forehead to her chin, making it hard for her to talk. "What's this?" she asked, examining her hand, which felt sticky as she drew it away from her face, covered in what looked like blood.

"Please lie still, ma'am," the attendant said, reaching over her to grab a large bandage. "Let me reinforce that wound," he added, placing something over the bandage already on the side of her face. "You've been injured… seriously. Please lie still."

"Where's my husband?" Gaby repeated, tears welling in her eyes. "What happened to us? Is he okay?"

"The police will fill you in on the details once we're at the hospital. We'll be there in a few minutes. Please, just try to stay calm."

Chapter 1

GABY DROPPED A TWENTY beside her plate of uneaten pancakes and hurried out of the Sunshine Café. Reading the unexpected note her waitress, Helen, had given her raised all of her old fears. She rushed across the road fronting Woodson Falls' small shopping area, making her way over the town green to Center Cemetery, where she could reflect on the note in peace and quiet. The oldest cemetery in Berkshire County, Center held the remains of men who had fought in the Civil War, the Revolutionary War, and as far back as the French and Indian Wars. The engravings on the thin, weathered stones were barely visible.

Gaby had returned to Woodson Falls to escape the memories of what had happened to her and Joe in the city. The sense of community and tradition here made her feel safe. Things like how the members of the town's Veterans Association had planted small American flags on the graves of the fallen men in this cemetery just a month ago, before Memorial Day. They'd be removed after Veterans Day in November, then stored until the following May.

Gaby sat on the stone wall surrounding the cemetery and gazed out toward Woodson Lake and the sparkling waterfall tucked into its far corner. A breeze scattered the dry leaves left from last autumn. She fingered the scar that ran from her left eye and along her cheek, usually hidden by the fall of her long black hair, as she reread the note the stranger had left for her:

> Joe wasn't who you thought he was. Better
> for you if you don't go down the same path.

When Gaby first spotted the strange man eating at the café counter a few months ago, she thought he looked familiar. She had only caught a glimpse of the tall, dark-haired man who had attacked her and her husband Joe after they left their favorite restaurant, where they had celebrated Joe's success in landing a big advertising account. As they strolled down the sidewalk arm-in-arm, heading toward their New York apartment, a man wielding a knife killed Joe and slashed Gaby's face. Then he jumped into the driver's seat of a white van and took off down the street. The police never caught him.

Gaby's scar was a constant reminder of that night and her loss. Now this note, confirming her worst fear—that whatever had prompted the attack on Joe had followed her from New York City to the sleepy rural town of Woodson Falls, Connecticut—had come just when she thought she might be ready to love again. The note was a stark reminder of how suddenly love could be taken from you, how empty life could become.

Following Joe's death and her own recovery from the knife wound and a broken ankle, shattered when Joe collapsed on her, Gaby had resigned her position as a professor of philosophy at Columbia University. She finished law school, was admitted to the bar, and became an attorney in Woodson Falls, specializing in estate planning and probate with a smattering of real estate. She renovated the cottage she inherited from her grandfather, reconnected with old friends, and acquired an emotional support dog, a beautiful German Sheprador named Katrina.

But what to do now?

After giving her the note from the stranger, Helen had suggested she forget it, but that was impossible. How could she forget something that had stirred up the anguish she thought she had finally put in the past?

Her dear friend Emma Larson, who usually manned the deli at Mike's Place, would just ask questions Gaby would be unable to answer. Besides, as much as Gaby loved her, Emma was an inveterate gossip and wouldn't be able to resist talking about the stranger's note to anyone who knew even a little about Gaby's past.

Nell Whitney, owner of Rainbows & Unicorns and Gaby's friend and legal mentor, was the most likely person Gaby could confide in, but Gaby feared that, like Helen, Nell would encourage her to tear up the note and forget about following it to wherever it was tempting to lead her.

And that left Matt Thomas, Woodson Fall's resident state trooper, who had helped her with cases that had begun at 16 Lakeview Terrace in the early spring and ended with the more recent case at 9 Donovan's Way just before Memorial Day. She and Matt had developed a friendship that had deepened over the past few months and was poised to turn into a romance, a step she felt ready to take… until she received this note. Having lost a spouse as well as his young daughter and unborn son to senseless violence, Matt would understand the distress the stranger's note had stirred in her. But something deep inside her resisted involving him. Solving this puzzle on her own might be the only way she could completely heal from her loss.

Gaby sat a while longer, staring out at the lake, then tucked the note into her purse. She decided to begin with Carl Grant, Joe's second-in-command at the ad agency. Perhaps he could shed some light on what Joe was involved with in the months preceding his death, other than the success in gaining the new ad account she and Joe had been celebrating.

Feeling a bit more settled now, having decided on a course of action, Gaby slid off the stone wall and headed back across the green toward her weathered Subaru, parked along the row of stores comprising Woodson Falls' shopping center. As she approached her car, the confidence she had just found drained away, replaced by a knot in the pit of her stomach at the sight of a white van with New York plates parked near the café.

Chapter 2

THE PHONE WAS RINGING when Gaby returned home from her shortened trip to town. She let Katrina out before picking up.

"Law offices, Gabriella Quinn speaking," she announced.

"Gaby, it's me. Matt."

"Are you okay? You sound worried."

"I am—about you. I was at the café this morning, right after you left. Helen told me you ran out without touching your breakfast. Is everything okay?"

"I'm fine."

"She told me about the note. You're not going to pursue this, are you?"

"Pursue what?" She really didn't want to get into an involved discussion about what she might do to solve the riddle of the attack on Joe.

"Come on, Gaby. Helen told me the note came from a stranger and seemed like a warning related to the attack on you and your husband."

And here I thought Emma was the gossip. "It's okay, Matt. Nothing to worry about."

"Please. Tell me what the note said. I want to help."

"Matt, you're a dear for wanting to help me, but this is something I need to work out for myself."

"Are you sure? You'll probably need to go to New York City at some point, and I know that's hard for you."

"I'll manage."

"Are you sure?" he asked again.

"Definitely."

"Promise to get me involved if you need to? Please?"

"Yes. I promise. I'll be okay," she reassured him. "I'm a big girl. I can take care of myself."

"I know that, but… You know I care about you."

"I do, and I care about you too. I promise I'll let you know if I need your help."

"Please do that."

"I will. Thanks for worrying about me, and for your willingness to help," she said, ending the call.

Sighing as she let Katrina back into the house after the dog's trip to the woods, Gaby brewed some tea and sat at the kitchen table. She wondered why the note had come now, so many years after the attack. Whatever it was that Joe might have uncovered or been involved in—if anything—couldn't still be an issue. And if it were something serious enough to kill him, Joe surely would have mentioned it to her and probably to whatever authorities should be involved.

But what if he had stumbled on something without realizing its significance? Regardless, why did she feel compelled to stir this particular hornet's nest, and possibly get stung, especially after being warned off?

She sipped her tea, pondering the possible answers to her own questions, beginning with the last. Why pursue this? What made her so certain that it was the right course to take, and to take alone?

After Joe was killed, Gaby experienced frequent panic attacks her therapist eventually attributed to post-traumatic stress disorder. The attacks had driven her from the city to this quiet corner of Connecticut, where she was surrounded by friends and supported by her canine companion. Kat had helped her through the bouts of sheer terror that diminished both in frequency and severity over time. But Gaby continued to over-react to every white van with New York plates she saw as well as any tall, dark-haired stranger she encountered. Either provoked a cold sweat and pounding heart very similar to her earlier panic attacks. She'd almost tumbled into such an attack when she spotted the white van as she left the cemetery.

The only way to put an end to these irrational responses was to get to the bottom of the lingering questions: Who would attack an advertising executive and a college professor? And why?

Chapter 3

GABY AND JOE had mixed with the same group of graduate students at Columbia. They gathered for lunch and the occasional after-class beer, but the two hadn't dated then. It took their chance meeting at Carl and Sylvia Grant's wedding several years later to rekindle their relationship. Joe had served as best man for his co-worker, Carl, whose bride, Sylvia, had invited Gaby to the wedding as her close friend and Columbia colleague. The two couples became fast friends, often attending events or having a simple supper together. Gaby and Joe married the year following Sylvia and Carl's wedding.

After Joe was killed, Carl helped Gaby deal with the advertising firm's human resources department to claim Joe's hefty life insurance as well as his sizable pension fund. Sylvia had recommended Gaby consider retaining Attorney Caryn Ellison, who helped with the administration of Joe's estate, transferring joint assets into Gaby's sole ownership and kindling her interest in a law career.

As a part of Joe's team at the advertising agency, Carl would have the best understanding of what Joe had been involved with before he was killed. Recalling that the agency usually reserved Wednesday afternoons for team meetings, Gaby timed her call to

Carl early the next day, a Wednesday, when she was most likely to find him in the office.

"Gaby!" Carl exclaimed when he picked up the line. "It's been too long! How've you been?"

"I'm doing well, Carl. And you? Sylvia? The kids?"

"All fine. We finally made the move out of the city after our oldest started school. Found a place in Greenwich. A better life for a growing family and not too bad a commute for me. Too much random violence in the city. Sorry. I know you already know that."

"Ah, yes," Gaby responded, a hitch in her voice. She wanted to veer off that subject, though it was at the heart of the reason she was calling. "I was wondering if you'd have time to talk with me in the next week or two. I'm trying to piece together what Joe was working on before the attack."

"So tragic! And right after we landed the Birch account, a real coup for him and for the agency. But didn't we talk that through after Joe was killed?"

"We did, but I think we might have missed something."

"Hmm… Okay." Carl paused. "I'm looking at my calendar. Wow! Only a week and a half until the long July Fourth weekend! Time sure does fly. I could do a late lunch this Friday if that would work for you."

"I'll make it work. Just tell me the time and place."

"How about the Park Avenue Tavern? Great for lunch, and it's close to Grand Central—I'm assuming you'll be coming in by train. That way, you won't have to traipse around the city, and we can both catch trains home after lunch."

"Sounds good. A late lunch, you said? Say one? One-thirty?"

"Let's make it one-thirty. That way, I can tie up whatever I'm working on."

"Thanks, Carl. See you then. Give my best to Sylvia."

"Will do. It'll be good to see you."

"Bye now."

"Bye, Gaby."

———

Gaby arrived at the Park Avenue Tavern a bit after Carl. The familiar tensing of her muscles and acceleration of her pulse began during the brief walk across the street from the train station to the restaurant. She felt better when she spotted Carl, who had secured a booth at the back of the brightly lit restaurant. Although the bar was busy with businessmen and women catching a late lunch or lingering over dessert, most of the booths had emptied of lunchtime customers.

"Thanks for meeting with me, Carl," Gaby said, pecking him on the cheek before taking her seat. "Sorry I'm late. Train was delayed." Carl seemed to have aged since Gaby had last seen him. She wondered whether the often-frenetic pace of the advertising business was taking its toll on the once-athletic man.

"No problem. I was able to wrap things up at the office earlier than expected, so I escaped while I could," Carl said with a smile.

After ordering and catching up a bit on each other's lives, Gaby explained the reason for her call, showing Carl the note she had received from the stranger.

"That had to have shaken you up," he said, handing it back to her.

"Big time. Some of my friends want me to ignore it, but this isn't going away. If it's ever going to, I need to get to the bottom of why Joe and I were attacked. I'm still having panic attacks, although they're less frequent now that I'm out of the city. Taking up jogging seems to have helped too. In any event, I'd like to put this all to rest if it's possible."

"I can understand that. So you think the attack on you and Joe was related to something he was working on?"

"Yes. I considered the possibility it was somehow related to my teaching at Columbia, but I just couldn't come up with anything. No angry students or parents I can recall. No offended colleagues either. Can you give me a clue? Maybe beginning with that new account that Joe was so happy about securing?"

"I've given this a lot of thought since you called. The approach we used on that account was new—different from anything done by ad agencies in the past."

"How so?"

"Did Joe talk about his work with you?"

"Not much. I usually knew what he was working on, but none of the specifics. Certainly not how he was approaching an assignment. We had decided early on not to let our careers take over our married life, so we tried to confine talk about work to broad outlines with few details. We shared big issues that were troubling either of us, of course. That's what makes me think Joe stumbled onto or into something he didn't recognize as significant."

"I get that. Sylvia and I handle our work lives much the same way. Here's the nutshell version of the approach we used with the new account. Advertising depends a great deal on repetition. Most multimedia campaigns use the same picture of the product accompanied by a hopefully memorable tag line, slogan or jingle. The assumption is, if a message is repeated often enough, it'll stick in a consumer's mind and prompt them to buy the product or service—whatever is being advertised. Joe thought redundancy worked, but there was a point at which a potential consumer turned off or tuned out a message, defeating the whole purpose of the ads.

"He had come up with this unique approach to a multimedia campaign we used for the first time with the Birch account. Joe explained it this way: Students in an art class usually draw or paint a model or still life posed in the center of a circle of students working at desks or easels. Each student sees the model from a somewhat different perspective. Each drawing or painting is an accurate portrayal of the model, but each reveals something unique about the subject. Taken together, the students' work creates a more complete picture of reality.

"Joe used the art class example to reveal various aspects of Birch's product, a cleaning solution, so the target audience would gain a fuller picture when exposed to print, television, radio and social media ads, all tied together with the same tag line. Joe thought this fuller picture or understanding of this client's product, in the Birch situation, its varied uses, would result in greater trust as consumers felt they 'knew' or better understood the product. He also thought some information was better conveyed over one medium than another. He said a good match of the message with the media being used was as important as the message."

"Shades of Marshall McLuhan," Gaby said with a smile. "Apparently it worked, but wasn't that a big gamble to take with a new account?"

"It could have been," Carl answered, "but Joe had tested his theory first."

"How?"

"We don't usually take on political campaigns, but we were approached by the campaign manager for a first-time candidate in a US senatorial race in New York and Joe wanted to use the opportunity as a test case before applying his theory with a larger, more traditional account. Joe and I usually collaborated on ad development, kicking ideas around, trying out approaches with the team before they were presented to a focus group and, ultimately, to a client. Joe didn't want to waste my time or the team's on this since it was just a theory, so he worked on it alone."

"Was it successful?"

"I'm guessing Joe felt it would work because he went ahead with applying the approach to the Birch account even though the would-be senator's campaign manager aborted the project before the preliminary ads could be shot and placed. I'm sure Joe requested the usual retainer before beginning the work. Our standard contract language covers the non-refundable retainer along with the option to decline to pursue implementation of the ad campaign that's developed.

"Joe said they decided not to proceed with the plan before the ads could be produced, due to cost constraints. You never know with these things. Money is always a good excuse if the client is concerned about the direction the campaign is headed.

"I tracked down a file Joe had developed on the project. It's probably meaningless, but I wanted to give it to you on the off chance it might help you figure out why you both were attacked. You could always contact the campaign manager for particulars. I think the same firm is handling Campbell's reelection campaign."

Chapter 4

GABY STARED out the train window, watching the scenery fly by as she tried to clear her mind of its racing thoughts about the stranger and the note he had left; clutching the still-unopened file folder Carl had given her. She had no intention of reading it on the train, afraid her emotions might not be able to handle whatever it contained.

Upon Gaby's return from the train station in nearby Pawling, New York, Kat greeted her enthusiastically when she opened the cottage door. Given her higher-than-usual alert level following her receipt of the stranger's note, Gaby was relieved that no one had broken into her house and Kat was okay. She rubbed the dog's head. "Just let me get into some running clothes, Kat. Be right back."

She put the folder and the note on her office desk, then headed to her bedroom, quickly changing clothes so she could spend some time with Kat after a long day away. The run would also release the nervous energy that threatened to boil over.

"Come on, Kat," she said. The dog perked her ears and bounded out the door as soon as it opened. Kat ran to the woods, did her business, then turned to wait for Gaby to come close before they both headed up the trail for their usual run around Beaver Pond.

The air was crisp, the sky a robin's egg blue before the sun set, the days much longer now, more than three months after Daylight Savings Time had moved the clocks forward.

As they neared home, Kat darted ahead of Gaby toward the police cruiser parked in front of the cottage. When Matt Thomas stepped out of his vehicle, Kat jumped up to greet him.

"Down, Kat," Gaby commanded as she drew near, panting a bit after the half-hour run. Kat obeyed, but continued to wag her tail vigorously and lean against the trooper.

"At least someone is glad to see me," Matt remarked, rubbing Kat's head.

"Hi there," Gaby said. "I'm happy to see you too. Just too sweaty to give you a hug."

Matt smiled. "I've been calling your home number all day…"

"I was in New York. Why don't we go inside to chat? Would you like a cup of coffee? A glass of wine?"

"Coffee would be great," he replied as the three headed toward the cottage door. "I'm going to be staying on duty into the night. The New Yorkers are here on weekends, and it can get a bit raucous into the late evening. Fights sometimes break out if people drink too much."

Gaby started a fresh pot of coffee, filled Kat's water bowl, and downed a bottle of Gatorade while she waited for the coffee to brew.

"Why were you calling?" she asked Matt, who had taken a seat at the kitchen table.

"I just wanted to apologize for pushing so hard the other day. I should know by now that you'd ask if you needed my help. I shouldn't have pushed."

"Funny," Gaby answered as she poured them each a mug of coffee and sat across from him. "I was going to apologize to you."

"For what?"

"For not letting you know what was going on. That wasn't fair. I should have just explained I didn't want what happened to Joe and me to interfere with… our friendship."

"Is that what this is?" Matt murmured.

"I don't know what 'this' is," Gaby answered softly. *Just what I'm hoping it could be,* the unspoken wish feeling too forward to voice.

"Hmm…" Matt gazed at Gaby while taking a sip of his coffee. "Could you just tell me what the note said? It obviously bothered you enough to run out of the café the other day without eating the breakfast you ordered."

Gaby got up from the table and retrieved the note from her office, handing it to Matt.

"Whoa!" he said after reading it. "This person is warning you off, and you wade in with both feet and no life preserver?"

"I went to New York to meet with Joe's right-hand man at the ad agency. He's an old friend. I wanted to find out what Joe was working on when he was killed. I had explored that avenue before, but back then I was focusing on his most recent account. The ad campaign for that one had been very successful. I thought there might be something else that would explain why we were attacked."

"So, did you learn anything?"

"Carl gave me a folder with Joe's notes on the project he was working on prior to the more recent one. He was testing a novel approach to an ad campaign. Carl thought the information might help."

"And?"

"I haven't looked at it yet. And no, I'm not jumping in with both feet. I'm just trying to make sense of what happened, if that's at all possible."

"Well, please be careful. Helen told me the stranger who gave her the note for you was working on the Haverson place. Think I'll mosie over there and see if I can chat with this 'stranger.' Find out who he is. I just want you to know," Matt said, getting up and putting his coffee cup in the sink. "I'm here if you need me. Happy to serve, as always," he added with a smile.

"Thank you. I really do appreciate that. And thanks for coming over."

"Sure. Thanks for the coffee. Gotta go, but I'll catch up with you later."

After Matt left, Gaby washed the coffee mugs and headed to the shower. She felt grubby after her run and the trip to New York City and back. She was grateful Carl's choice of a restaurant for their meeting didn't involve her walking too far into the heart of the city.

As she dried off from the shower, she wondered whether the folder Carl had given her would contain anything helpful but, as much as she was tempted to delve in immediately, she decided instead to relax with the book she was reading and go to bed early. Tomorrow was another day.

Gaby started her weekend with a leisurely breakfast, opting not to take her usual morning run. She brought her second cup of coffee into her office and stared for a while at the unopened folder on her desk.

She took a deep breath. "Here goes!"

Opening the folder, she smiled a bit to see Joe's familiar neat printing. He had majored in marketing as an undergraduate at Northeastern University, but minored in graphic design. His neat printing reflected that training.

The first few pages in the folder were organized, cataloging the information Joe would be seeking as he embarked on the ad campaign. These notes followed the rubric used by journalists, asking who, what, when, where, why and how. Once Joe had the answers to those basic questions, Gaby assumed he would select which angles to pursue in more depth as he developed a comprehensive advertising campaign for the would-be senator.

Leafing ahead in the folder, Gaby saw that, true to form, Joe's work became more scattered as his creativity kicked in. There were frequent departures from the printed answers to the stock questions, arrows pointing to notes on the side of the page or on the reverse. Some sketches, more detailed questions. Words or phrases circled or underscored. Slips of paper with sketches or phrases apparently related to the project. Deciphering these later notes might provide some clues to why the candidate stopped his work with Joe before the ad campaign could be launched.

Now, six years later, Gaby was aware that the candidate, Arnold Campbell, was seeking reelection, his initial campaign for the Senate seat successful even without Joe's help.

It made no sense that, all these years later, the note the stranger had left for Gaby was related to Joe's work with Campbell. But if not this, what?

Chapter 5

GABY LOOKED AGAIN at the stranger's note propped against her desk lamp. Had she veered off in the wrong direction? Seeking clues in Joe's work rather than in what she knew about him, or thought she knew? The note seemed more directed at her connection with Joe than his suspended involvement with a political campaign.

When Carl had mentioned Joe's solo work on Campbell's efforts to win one of the two New York seats in the US Senate, she thought it possible that, in testing out his new approach to the design of the overall advertising, Joe had uncovered some deep dark secret that could have cost the candidate the election and possibly sent him to prison. After all, it was Joe who had been killed, clearly the target of the attack. Now that Campbell was running to keep his Senate seat, he might be worried that Joe had told his wife about the secret and she would reveal it publicly and ruin Campbell's chances of reelection.

But sitting here in the quiet of her cottage and the comfort of this small town she'd made her home, Gaby wondered if there was something about Joe she didn't know, perhaps aware of but never realizing its significance. Maybe it was best to pursue both angles: comb through Joe's notes on Arnold Campbell in search of possible clues to some mystery he would do anything to keep secret, as well as think through all she knew about Joe that might have prompted someone to kill him and now threaten her.

Putting aside the folder detailing Joe's work on the Campbell campaign, Gaby grabbed a new legal pad and began jotting down all she knew about her husband.

He had grown up in South Boston, the oldest of three boys in a middle-class family. She'd met them all. His mother was a high school English teacher, his father, a CPA with a large accounting firm. Family get-togethers were a bit tumultuous—lots of kidding and rough-housing among the boys—but she always felt welcomed, even before she and Joe had married and more so afterward.

Joe had graduated summa cum laude from Northeastern University, then entered Columbia's MBA program. Having done an internship for a small advertising firm in Boston between his junior and senior years at Northeastern, he loved the work— enjoyed the client contacts and the creative challenges it involved.

His faculty adviser and his supervisor at the ad firm both sent glowing recommendations for Joe. Along with his undergraduate GPA and GMAT scores, those recommendations clinched his admission to the MBA program. Columbia offered him a merit scholarship carrying full tuition, enabling him to attend school full-time although he worked odd jobs on weekends in order to eat and pay his portion of the rent on a loft apartment he shared with three other guys on his learning team at Columbia.

Quickly recruited by a mid-sized advertising firm in New York City in need of his skill in the design of social media-based advertising campaigns, Joe began working there right after graduating. He rose steadily in the ranks and became the team leader for a small group that included Carl Grant, who Joe had recruited to the firm. He had regular hours for the most part and did some traveling for work, often involving an overnight stay, but nothing that interfered with their life as a young married couple.

Between Joe's salary and her own, they were comfortable financially. Both tended to be prudent about expenditures, and they never fought about money—an issue that over the years had doomed many marriages among their circle of acquaintances.

Joe was a devoted Red Sox, Celtics and New England Patriots fan, preferred wine or beer over hard liquor, had smoked a bit in college, but not after he graduated. He enjoyed movies and the theater, but not opera. He played racquetball with some coworkers three times a week and a low-stakes, friendly poker game once a month with some college friends.

Joe claimed to be middle-of-the-road politically, liberal on social issues but conservative on financial ones. He declined to declare a party preference, registering as an independent voter. He voted in most elections but seemed minimally interested in politics, so his decision to take on the Campbell campaign had struck Gaby as odd. Why get involved with something he cared little about? Still, you could say the same about the cleaning products he had touted in the Birch campaign. Accepting the challenge of working on the would-be senator's run for office probably offered Joe the opportunity to test his theory about integrating several perspectives on the candidate in an unfolding ad campaign.

And that was about it. Nothing popped out, no threads she could pull on to see what unraveled. Nothing. So, it was back to the folder Carl had given her and its notes on the aborted political campaign.

Gaby put down the legal pad and went into the kitchen to prepare a late lunch. Then she took a walk with Kat, mulling over all she remembered about Joe over their years together.

Returning to her office after her walk, Gaby pulled the legal pad with her notes about Joe toward her and began circling items that might be worth exploring in greater depth. Several things might deserve a deeper dive, though Gaby was reluctant to find anything that might tarnish her memories of Joe. Still, Matt's concern about her safety, underscoring the implicit threat in the stranger's note, was generating those familiar internal pings signaling potential danger.

She couldn't remember just what Joe's brothers—Stephen and Richard—did for a living. Joe exchanged texts and emails with both of them fairly regularly. She assumed they were just keeping tabs on one another, but what if the brothers were involved with something that diverted Joe from the straight-and-narrow?

Was there some connection to the odd jobs he worked on weekends while at Columbia? It seemed far-fetched, but perhaps she should "push the envelope" to see if there was anything of substance to be explored. If the odd jobs weren't related to his family ties, were they connected with his New York roommates? Again, a stretch, but that's what this ruminating was about. Trying to uncover a clue that may or may not be there and may or may not relate to the stranger's note.

The phone rang. "Law offices, Gabriella Quinn speaking," she announced, continuing to stare at the yellow pad.

"Oh Gaby," the gravelly voice of Winston Pinkham, her long-time client, said. "I'm so very sorry to disturb you on the weekend."

"Mr. Pinkham! No problem. You sound worried. What's going on? How can I help you?"

"Oh my dear, I *am* worried. I did a stupid, stupid thing, and I'm not quite sure how to fix it. Do you think you could come over sometime tomorrow? It can wait until Monday, but if it's at all possible, I'd like to see you before then."

"Of course. It's a bit late," she answered, glancing at the clock, "but I can pop over now if you like."

"No, no. Sometime tomorrow would be soon enough. That wouldn't be a bother?"

"Not at all. Can you tell me what this is about?"

"I think I need to show you. It's to do with the subdivision."

"Sunrise Hills? Wasn't the subdivision plan approved earlier this month?"

"Yes. And I know I'll need to put up a bond for the road before I can offer the lots for sale. I was working on that when I discovered…"

"Yes?"

"Oh Gaby, I'm so worried. Thank you for picking up the call… for being there. What time do you think you can come tomorrow?"

"I'll be there right after church. A bit past eleven. Is that okay?"

"Wonderful. Thank you so much, Gaby. You have a lovely evening."

"You as well, Mr. Pinkham. Whatever this is, we'll sort it out together."

Chapter 6

GABY LEFT Woodson Falls Congregational Church following the ten o'clock service and headed to Winston Pinkham's home at 2 Sunrise Trail. Pinkham had been one of her first clients when she opened her law practice. Over the years, he'd revised his will several times and asked for Gaby's help with other matters, including the slow progress of the subdivision he was creating on land adjoining his home.

Never married and with only a cousin or two, the eighty-nine-year-old added and removed beneficiaries from the various iterations of his will as the mood struck him. Pinkham had asked Gaby to be his executor as well as act for him under a power of attorney if he was unable to manage his affairs. She knew it would be a complicated estate to administer, given the number of beneficiaries Pinkham had named in the latest revision of his will, to say nothing of the issues with the subdivision that still needed to be resolved.

Despite the light breeze that ruffled her hair as she made her way to her car, the gathering clouds signaled a probable rainstorm ahead. The day might end up being too wet to do the gardening she'd planned for later in the afternoon.

Knocking on Pinkham's door to let him know she had arrived, she entered the dated living room, its walls papered in a dusty rose motif, both the wallpaper and colonial furniture in contrast with the oriental rugs scattered on the oak floor. Pinkham wasn't in his usual spot, sitting in a worn wingback chair. On the end table next to it, a thread of smoke rose from a cigarette left smoldering in an ashtray already filled with butts.

Pinkham's oxygen concentrator was chugging away, so Gaby followed the tubing to find her client in a spare bedroom he used as an office. He was standing at an ancient roll-top desk, oxygen cannula in his nose, shuffling papers and shaking his head. A large, yellowed and very elaborate genealogy chart titled "Pinkham" hung on the wall above the desk. In past visits, Pinkham had told Gaby of his interest in tracing his family tree. Having no siblings or immediate family except for the far-flung cousins, he instead surrounded himself with past relations. He found comfort in feeling connected to something larger than himself, even if only long-deceased family members.

"There you are!" Gaby called in greeting.

"Oh, Gaby. Thanks so much for making time for me. Let's go sit in the parlor so I can tell you my problem."

Following the tubing back into the living room, they each sat in their accustomed spots, he in the wing-backed chair, she on the sofa next to him. Pinkham stubbed out the still-burning cigarette but didn't light another.

"You seemed so troubled when you called yesterday, Mr. Pinkham," Gaby began.

"My dear, you've known me a long time. Can we dispense with the 'Mister'? My friends call me Win. Humor an old man, dear. Call me Win, please."

"Okay… Win," Gaby continued, "Can you tell me what's going on? You said it had something to do with the Sunrise Hills subdivision you're creating?"

"Oh, Gaby. I feel so stupid, and my reputation will be in tatters, although that's the least of it. What I've done is unforgivable and, worse, I don't think it can be undone. I've tried to sort it out, but I can't. I'm hoping you can help me find a way out of the mess I've made."

"Why not begin at the beginning and tell me what this is about? What has you so upset? I'll do what I can to help you work things out once I know what's happened."

Taking the nasal prongs from his nose and allowing the cannula to hang from his neck, Pinkham lit a cigarette and inhaled deeply while Gaby sat there shaking her head. Despite his significant chronic obstructive pulmonary disease, Pinkham had been unwilling or unable to break his lifelong habit of smoking.

"You really shouldn't be doing that, you know," she said. "It isn't just the smoking, which aggravates your lungs and affects your breathing. I realized a long time ago that it's a habit you're unlikely to stop at this point in your life, as you've told me many times. I've done a bit of research and learned that oxygen is itself not combustible, but it does support combustion, making a small fire bigger and possibly out of control. With the concentrator delivering pure oxygen to that tubing, the small flame from your lighter could turn into an uncontrollable fire. The very least you might do is turn the concentrator off when you feel you need to smoke."

Pinkham nodded, offering a meek smile, but kept smoking while the concentrator continued to chug away.

"Now, what's this all about?"

"You know I've been involved with the Woodson Falls Land Trust practically all my adult life. I used to help with clearing trails on newly acquired land, maintaining the existing trails, leading hikes, and the like. I was tapped to be president of the group at one time—served for many years in that capacity—then, because of my long career in the banking industry, I was asked to be the land trust's development coordinator."

He took a long drag on his cigarette, then continued. "I've been managing financial matters for the trust for many, many years. People who want to keep the rural look and feel of Woodson Falls have been very generous in donating not only land, but also appreciated stock, payouts from retirement plans they don't need for their day-to-day living, that sort of thing. It's been my practice to invest the financial donations in conservative instruments, preserving capital while generating income needed to support the maintenance of land trust properties as well as, on occasion, office operations."

"Okay. What went wrong?"

"Let me begin at the beginning. I hired Blackberry Hill Engineering to plan the Sunrise Hills subdivision last December, months before I had you make the changes to my will providing a discount on two lots to friends who offered to help me with the subdivision process along the way. You met them when you attended that planning and zoning meeting last month. I never imagined there would be so many costs involved in something that seemed so simple at the start, or that the whole process would take so long to complete. But there I was, committed to following through in hopes of making enough of a profit on the development of the land to live out my final years."

"I've heard that any land development is costly, and I understood from your land use attorney that it's a difficult plot of land. I imagine the work to create the subdivision cost more than you had bargained for. Especially after we discovered how both the engineering firm and your friends, Adam and Bud, were delaying the process."

"Yes, indeed. And I'm so glad you intervened like you did when that happened. Your talking to both the engineers and my friends got the whole thing moving through the approvals.

"Would you believe?" Pinkham barked, shaking his head. "After all that, Adam and Bud have been badgering me, insisting I leave them those lots outright through my will or grant them each a deeper discount than the twenty percent I've already offered. Between them and the head of the local land trust, I feel like I'm in the middle of a tug of war, and anything I do is going to disappoint someone. But it's *my* land to do with as I please. I shouldn't have to justify my actions to anyone. The nerve of them!" Pinkham's vehement outburst set off a coughing fit.

Once it had passed, he said, "So getting back to the costs of the whole process of subdividing my land… 'In for a penny, in for a pound,' as they say. Once begun, there didn't seem to be a way to stop the work to create the subdivision. I'd already spent a good deal on the process and felt I needed to finish it in order to at least recoup my expenses, if not make a profit." Pinkham took another long drag on his cigarette, then stubbed it out.

"Along the way, I found it necessary to liquidate some of my investments to pay the ongoing expenses related to the subdivision," Pinkham continued. "I've always been very careful to pay my bills as soon as I receive them. I've known folks who let them go until the end of the month but then forget them entirely, racking up costly penalties."

"I know," Gaby interjected. "It's a problem some of my elderly clients have. Is that what happened to you?"

"Oh no. Nothing so simple," Pinkham responded, lighting another cigarette while the oxygen concentrator continued to chug along. "A few weeks before work got started on Sunrise Hills, the land trust began a major development campaign with the goal of raising a half-million dollars by the end of this year for the purchase of a large tract of land. A benefactor of the trust had pledged to match the donations up to that amount—essentially doubling the funds we were hoping to raise."

"Wow! I knew there were a lot of wealthy people in Woodson Falls, but that's super-generous."

"People who are interested in conserving land will do just about anything to accomplish their goal. We're lucky here in Woodson Falls to have so many people who support our cause. Not just the wealthy either. A lot of young people get involved with doing the work to maintain our holdings, which is as vital as conserving the land."

"I can see that. But back to your concerns," Gaby said, hoping Pinkham would finally circle around to the core issue that was troubling him.

Chapter 7

"Just as I've been careful to pay my bills on time, I've taken pains to separate the management of land trust funds from my own financial transactions," Pinkham continued. "Despite that, somewhere along the way, I ended up depositing land trust donations into one or another of my personal accounts and even paid a few of my own bills from land trust funds. I only noticed the discrepancy when I went to pay the bond for the road construction in Sunrise Hills so I could begin selling the lots."

"Oh, that *is* a problem," Gaby ventured, "but surely your accountant or bookkeeper can help you sort it out."

"I've been too embarrassed to ask them, hoping I could get to the bottom of it on my own. But I seem to have muddled things so badly, it's next to impossible to track down my errors and reverse them. If only the land trust's treasurer hadn't resigned suddenly, perhaps this wouldn't have happened. But he did—moving to Texas, of all places—and this mess is a consequence of that. I take full responsibility for what happened, but..."

"Why don't you outline the situation with the land trust for me?" Gaby asked. "What are your responsibilities as developmental coordinator for the land trust, and how has the treasurer's resignation affected those responsibilities?"

Pinkham took a long drag on his cigarette before stubbing it out. Tenting his hands under his chin, he continued, "As good a place to start as any, I suppose, if you have the time."

"Of course, Mr. Pinkh—Win," Gaby said, leaning toward him to convey her interest in what was worrying him. "I can't leave you so troubled. I want to help you work this out." She had learned early on in her practice that elderly clients often felt the need to take a circuitous route to describe what often was a relatively straightforward problem. The extra time it might take to get a good sense of the issue Pinkham was presenting to her was a small price to pay for the peace of mind it might likely bring her client.

"You are a dear soul, Gaby. I don't know what I would do without you," Pinkham replied, pausing to light yet another cigarette and taking a long drag before continuing. "We're a small trust with an even smaller staff, all part time. Our executive director, Percival Conway—he prefers to be addressed as Val, but I stick with Percival—oversees day-to-day operations.

"Hal Jordan is the land conservation manager and monitors the status of our properties to ensure no one has encroached on them, as well as the status of the trail system we've developed over the years. Volunteers assist Hal with those endeavors when they're available.

"Then there's our secretary, Hilda Morrow. In addition to the usual administrative duties, she's also responsible for encouraging active membership in the land trust and planning such activities as meetings, hikes, our annual dinner, things like that. Volunteers handle all the rest, including the management of land trust funds.

"We maintain two checking accounts: the operating account and the development account. The former treasurer—his name is Alfred Prunagle—has been responsible for the operating account, using it to pay everyday bills such as rent for our office space, electricity, wages and the like. Smaller donations to the land trust—one hundred dollars or less—are deposited into that account. Those donations usually are sufficient to meet our ongoing operational costs. If more is required, I transfer income earned on investments from the development account into the operating account.

"I manage the development account, which is used to fund occasional purchases of land, like the large tract of land I mentioned earlier, although most of the land trust holdings have been donated outright. As I said before, the development account is used mostly to pay costs related to maintaining land trust properties. You'd be surprised how expensive it is to manage them, even with all the volunteer help we have."

"I imagine so, but that's what makes Woodson Falls so special. All that open space really preserves the rural feel of the town," Gaby ventured.

"And that's the whole raison d'être of the land trust," Pinkham responded with the first smile she'd seen since she arrived. "Good to know we've been successful."

Gaby returned his smile, then said, "Go on."

"Alfred also was responsible for picking up and depositing donations into the appropriate account—operational or development—based on the size of the donation, recording the donations, then sending a list of donors to Hilda, our secretary, to acknowledge. He used the same procedure for donations in excess of one hundred dollars, which he deposited into the development account. Donations of financial instruments—stocks, bonds and the like—have been directed to me, and I do the work necessary to transfer the instrument into our development account with the bank."

"Okay," Gaby said, signaling that she understood how the financial workings of the land trust were handled. "So how did the treasurer's resignation affect things?"

"Well, my dear, it all landed in my lap, at least until some-one steps forward and volunteers to take over Alfred's position," Pinkham said, stabbing his half-finished cigarette into the ashtray. A thin trail of smoke from the still-smoldering cigarette rose from the receptacle.

"As a safeguard for land trust funds, any disbursement from either the operating or the development account requires two signa-tures from trust officers," Pinkham continued. "Since Alfred was aware I don't get out much, he signed a good number of checks for both accounts before he left, so I wouldn't be troubled to find an officer to sign the checks I would need to write."

Gaby sat back and rolled her eyes. "You know…"

"Yes, yes. I know that wasn't prudent. It was a kind gesture on his part, but now I regret agreeing to it. I should have just declined to pick up Alfred's responsibilities, especially with the Sunrise Hills business going on at the same time." Pinkham lit another cigarette. "As donations landed in my mailbox—far more than usual due to our fundraising campaign—I fell behind. And, I fear, having opened up the envelopes containing the donations and my own statements, I muddled them together.

"Alfred did all of his recordkeeping on his computer, but I don't have one, nor do I want to get one—or one of those new-fangled cell phones either, for that matter. I prefer maintaining accounts by hand using the information from the paper monthly state-ments I receive in the mail or directly from the donation forms to keep track of it all. Before leaving for Texas, Alfred did give me a printed copy of transactions beginning in January of this year and continuing through the end of March, including both donations and expenditures. I haven't been able to keep up with the records. Started to, but then I fell behind.

"I'm less worried about untangling the few donations of stocks and bonds we've received since Alfred's departure. Any financial institution worth its salt tracks transactions involving the conversion of one type of financial instrument into cash or another investment. But what went on here—between the land trust accounts and my own—has proved much too difficult to sort out."

"Oh, dear," Gaby said. "What can I do to help?"

"To be honest, Gaby dear," Pinkham said, "I wish I could throw the whole mess into your lap, but that's hardly fair. What do you think I should do?"

"I think," Gaby said, knowing she would likely rue her next words, "I think you should throw the whole mess into my lap, and I'll see what I can do to untangle your affairs from those of the land trust."

The relief Gaby saw on Pinkham's face was so evident she knew she wouldn't be able to back out, nor would she want to. "Why don't we go back into your office to gather the papers I'll need to work on this?"

"If I do that," Pinkham said with a forlorn shake of his head, "I fear I'll regret handing all that mess to you and, instead, slide back into the muddle I've made. No, I trust you completely to gather up everything on my desk. I don't do much in the office other than land trust and personal financial transactions anyway, but anything extraneous would be safe in your hands. There should be one of those accordion files there as well you can use to carry the papers. One of those brown manila folders that expand."

Gaby left Sunrise Trail with a file bulging with the papers Pinkham had been fretting about, along with a stack of paperwork that wouldn't fit into the accordion file she had found in his office. While she already had an even larger stack of work in her office in need of attention, the extra burden of attempting to resolve Pinkham's dilemma would occupy her mind for quite a while. Perhaps making her way through his paperwork would divert her attention from ruminations about the meaning of the stranger's note.

Arriving back at her cottage in the late afternoon, she dumped Pinkham's papers on her desk, had a quick lunch, then changed to go for a run around Beaver Pond with Kat before it rained.

Chapter 8

AFTER AN EARLY MORNING RUN on Monday, Gaby took her second cup of coffee into her office. She moved Pinkham's mess of papers aside for now, separating these from the pile of case folders she had left on the desk last Thursday, before Friday's trip to New York. She had no idea how long it might take her to sort through Pinkham's intertwined personal and land trust documents. Perhaps it would be best to work on the rest of her cases before attacking the pile she'd brought home from Sunrise Trail.

Gaby felt a deep need to take some leisure time after the traumas she had encountered at 16 Lakeview Terrace and 9 Donovan's Way, never mind the warning contained in the stranger's note. Her goal was to clear her desk before the long Fourth of July holiday weekend, then use the upcoming four-day stretch to renew her soul. Perhaps even take a few long swims with Kat out to the islands in the middle of Woodson Lake if the water was warm enough.

Gaby had scheduled appointments the following week with three clients who had called wanting to make changes to their wills. A review of the existing documents and any notes she had made would help reacquaint her with these clients' various issues ahead of those meetings.

Another client wanted to deed a large piece of property in Prescott to a beneficiary he had previously named in his will rather than leave the gift to be transferred upon his death. That would require drafting a quitclaim deed as well as revising this client's will.

She also needed to draft a contract of sale for yet another client who was selling her house before moving back to the city. And she had just heard from a new client who was seeking help with a Medicaid application for her father, and a couple new to town who were seeking advice on placing the house they'd just purchased into a residential trust.

Much of this work would be handled by a paralegal in an established law office, but her solo practice didn't generate enough income to take one on, even part-time. Gaby also felt immersing herself in the details of her clients' legal issues gave her the opportunity to detect and address any potential problems before they morphed into actual ones.

Working steadily over the next few days, Gaby made it close to the bottom of the pile of work, where she encountered the file Carl had given her. She had wanted to call Arnold Campbell's campaign manager, as Carl had suggested, to see if she could learn more about why the proposed advertising scheme Joe created for them wasn't used in the candidate's first run for the Senate seat. This was as good a time as any to do just that.

Bart Owens, Campbell's campaign manager, picked up the telephone after Gaby explained to the receptionist who she was and what she was calling about.

"We were so sorry to learn that Joe had been killed. You have my heartfelt condolences on your loss. I'm sure you still mourn his death, even so many years later. Joe was such a great guy—brilliant, easy to work with, and a straight shooter, qualities hard to find in this business. It pained us to abandon the advertising campaign he devised. We just didn't have the funds. Joe's suggested approach really provided a unique tactic that would have highlighted the assets Arnie would bring to his work in the US Senate."

"So it was insufficient funds that caused you to abandon the campaign Joe had developed?" Gaby asked.

"Absolutely! A first-time candidate like Arnie always has a harder time raising donations than does an established candidate the voters already know. We were fortunate to get him elected on the shoestring budget we had back then. This time around, it's been much easier to build a significant war chest. If Joe still was alive, we would have reached out to him to develop a revised advertising campaign to support Arnie's reelection, even knowing that, as a rule, his firm didn't handle political campaigns."

"Can I ask why you chose my husband's firm to design the advertisements for Senator Campbell's first run for office?"

"No problem. It seemed to us, looking over the ads his firm designed, that they valued a message that reflected diversity, especially in the people depicted in those ads. That resonated with Arnie's belief in the importance of attracting a diverse base of support but also with his desire to advocate for increased diversity in all aspects of human endeavor. We felt that the advertising campaign should both reflect and emphasize those values as a critical issue being addressed in Arnie's campaign messages."

"So, there was no other reason for backing out? No other reason for stopping your work with my husband?" Gaby probed further.

"Not at all. Honestly. It was like falling into a bed of roses when Joe agreed to work with us. We couldn't have been happier with his proposed approach to Arnie's message, which could easily be amplified given the senator's successes during his first six years in office. He was able to make a good bit of progress on the issues he ran on."

"I'm glad. Thanks for taking my call and answering my questions," Gaby said.

"I'm sorry, Mrs. Quinn. If you don't mind my asking, why are you calling us at this late date about our work with your husband?"

"Back when Joe was killed, the police assumed it was a random attack. Something's come up, making me question that, and I've been wondering if there were any issues surrounding Joe's work with Senator Campbell's initial campaign. You've assured me there aren't any. I'll explore some other avenues, but like the police back then, I'm probably unlikely to uncover anything.

"In any event, thank you so much for taking the time to talk with me. And good luck to Senator Campbell on his bid for reelection."

"Thanks, Mrs. Quinn. And good luck to you as well in your search for answers," Owens said before hanging up.

Taking a break for a quick lunch, Gaby brought the pile of Pinkham's papers into the kitchen so she could begin sorting through them after eating. It was a beautiful, cloudless summer day, so Gaby let Kat outside and brought her salad and iced tea to the small table and chairs set on the patio next to the garden. She delighted in the variety of plants there, no longer crowded and fighting for space after her hard work in restoring the spacious garden. The lively display of blues, pinks and yellows from the flowers in bloom brought a smile to her face. She felt content, pleased with the work she had completed. Having returned from the woods across the road, Kat lolled next to her, enjoying the sunshine.

Gaby's thoughts went back to her conversation with the campaign manager, who had characterized Joe as a "straight shooter." He was indeed. It was a quality she had been attracted to when they were first dating, especially given her specialization in ethics, one of the several areas of philosophical inquiry. If Joe had encountered some corrupt behavior on Campbell's part, prompting Joe's abrupt departure from the campaign, he would have told Gaby about it. They may not have shared every minor detail of their work lives, but a big issue like corruption was something Joe surely would have discussed with her.

Guess I can cross that off my list of possible answers to the stranger's note. Except… What if Joe didn't recognize the importance of something he discovered in his work with Campbell? And if he had, how ever would I be able to unearth it? Probably a dead end, for many reasons.

Once she and Kat returned to the cottage after a peaceful half hour of sunshine, Gaby began sorting Pinkham's papers into piles, one for his personal affairs and the other for land trust business. Pinkham had begun juggling both the treasurer and development coordinator duties sometime in April, and the volume of papers reflected the nearly three months of accumulated business. Pinkham had opened the many envelopes addressed to the land trust marked "Save Meadow Ridge" but, for the most part, hadn't removed or deposited the checks inside.

She could see how confusing the situation had gotten for dear old Pinkham. No wonder he thought he'd slipped mentally! The extent of the paperwork piled on the kitchen table was mind-boggling for her, and she was used to dealing with lots and lots of paper. What was that movie about law school? *The Paper Chase?* This was worse than anything she'd encountered in her law career or even as a doctoral student working on her dissertation. What a mess!

Beginning with the pile of Pinkham's personal papers, Gaby began sorting them by date, starting with the month of April and moving on through June. Although Pinkham had claimed to be on top of his bills, she found several unopened envelopes clearly containing bills that were now overdue by two months. That is, unless Pinkham had set up automatic payments through his bank, which she doubted.

Once his personal papers had been organized, she turned to the land trust paperwork—at least double in amount compared to

Pinkham's personal correspondence. She set aside the donations as she came across them, then organized the remaining papers by date as she had with her client's.

Pinkham said he was concerned he'd used land trust funds to pay bills related to the Sunrise Hills subdivision, so it was most important to sort this out first by examining the bank statements for each of the land trust accounts. It looked like he had, indeed, used three checks from the development account for various bills related to the subdivision. It would be harder to sort out any deposits of land use funds made to Pinkham's personal account, but that could wait until next week.

She was getting cross-eyed, looking at the mountains of paperwork spread across the kitchen table. Dinner would have to be served on a tray tonight… unless she headed to the café.

Chapter 9

"LAW OFFICES—"

Matt interrupted her standard opening. "It's me, Gaby. Matt. How are you?"

"Overworked and underpaid," she said with a chuckle. "You?"

"Same. I was wondering if you'd be free for supper? I'm bushed and don't feel like cooking. I was going to pick up something at Mike's Place, but it'd be nice to have company at the café instead. That is, unless you've already eaten or have other plans."

"Neither and, yes, I'm free. My kitchen table is covered with paperwork for a client, and I was just thinking about what I was going to do for dinner."

"Meet you at the café then in, say, half an hour? In addition to looking for company, I want to pick your brain about the Fourth here in Woodson Falls."

"See you then."

Gaby changed from her jeans and sweaty t-shirt into something a bit more presentable before feeding Kat and hopping into her Subaru. She was glad to have a reason to stop working on Pinkham's dilemma, as well as a solution to her indecision about dinner. She wondered idly what Matt wanted to know about the upcoming holiday, but was happy to be seeing him after their brief encounter the previous Friday. She hoped he wouldn't grill her about what she planned to do about the stranger's note. At this point, she hadn't a clue.

Matt was sitting in a booth, scrutinizing the café menu, when she arrived. He looked up at Gaby with those piercing blue eyes and her heart skipped a beat.

"There you are! Thanks so much for joining me. Want an herbal tea?"

"Sure. How are you, besides bushed?" she asked.

"Doing okay, I guess. So, what's going on with all the files on your kitchen table?"

"A longtime client of mine, Winston Pinkham, is concerned he's inadvertently mixed up personal funds with those of the land trust he's associated with. He wants to remedy the situation and reverse any errors he may have made, restoring funds owed to the land trust as quickly as possible. I offered to unravel the mess for him. And it is a mess. But he's old and so worried that I fear he isn't thinking straight."

"Alzheimer's?"

"No. Or at least I don't think so. He just took on too much and was worried about other things. Lost track. It's complicated."

"Nice of you to do that," Matt said, smiling.

"Mr. Pinkham, well, Win, I guess. He's asked me to call him that, like his friends do. He's like a grandfather to me, and I couldn't bear seeing him so distressed."

"What'll it be?" the waitress asked as she approached their booth.

Matt spoke up. "An herbal tea for Ms. Quinn, and I'll stick with water for now. We haven't looked at our menus yet."

"Fine. Take your time. I'll bring your beverages right over, and then you can give me a wave when you're ready to order. Name's

Suzie, handsome," she said, giving Matt's shoulder a squeeze before turning to greet some newcomers.

Gaby rolled her eyes. "So what do you need to know about the Fourth?"

"Just trying to get a feel for what the holiday is like here, it being my first."

Gaby smiled. "Aw, and here I thought you were just looking for an excuse to have some company."

"That too," Matt said, smiling back.

"So, the Fourth. I imagine you already know about the parade," Gaby began after they had consulted their menus and Suzie had brought their beverages.

"Yeah. The mayor filled me in on the broad strokes, particularly the parade. I've got some troopers coming in to manage traffic while it's on."

"So," Gaby began, "I'm sure Mayor Dunleavy told you that the town celebrates the Fourth on a Sunday, even though the holiday is actually on Tuesday this year. It's a town tradition. Even if the Fourth falls on a Saturday, the parade and fireworks always happen on Sunday. As far as the parade goes, there'd be hardly anyone to watch if it weren't for the out-of-towners who arrive early, mostly to secure front-row seats for the fireworks later. Pretty much the entire town participates in the parade—scouts, sports teams, clubs, veterans, whatever. The main attraction, though, is the fireworks display out in the middle of the lake, which begins once the sun sets."

"Ready?" Suzie asked, clearly not waiting for their wave.

"I'll have the Thai salad, no cheese, dressing on the side, please," Gaby answered.

"Chicken pot pie for me, Suzie."

"Coming right up, hon!" Suzie said with a wink meant for the trooper.

"Must be a great day for a place like this," Matt commented to Gaby, looking around at the tables that were filling with early evening diners. The café had been decorated in anticipation of the upcoming holiday, with red, white and blue carnations, along with two small American flags in the vases on each table.

"Absolutely! The café is packed, and Emma, over at Mike's Place, has taken to making assorted sandwiches-to-go ahead of time to keep up with the demand. Even Nell stays open, only closing the shop once the sun is ready to set. She'll be joining me to watch the fireworks—one of our 'traditions,'" Gaby said with a smile, air quotes around "traditions."

Their waitress came over with their meals. "Anything else I can get for you folks?"

"Gab?" asked Matt.

She shook her head. "I'm fine for now, thanks."

"If you'll just top off my water, we'll be all set, Suzie," Matt said with a smile.

They ate in silence for a while, then Matt asked, "Any problems I should be on the alert for?"

"Sometimes a tipsy boater gets too close to the fireworks action, but the lake patrol is pretty good at putting a stop to that sort of thing. The real problem can be with private parties shooting off fireworks illegally—and sometimes hazardously. Those will be the calls you'll be responding to, far into the night. You might want to get to bed early on Saturday or sleep in next Sunday morning, or both. You'll be up late Sunday night for sure."

"Good advice. Thanks."

They continued eating, then Matt asked, "Any plans for the holiday?"

"Some much needed R&R," Gaby answered. "Joe's family invited me to their usual holiday gathering. Nice, but I really don't want to battle the traffic up to Framingham and back. I'll touch base with them sometime after the weekend. My parents are in Europe on one of their research ventures—more vacation than research, I suspect, but they've earned it. I imagine you'll be on duty most of the time, no?"

"Yeah. No rest for the weary," Matt said, leaning back into the booth. He'd polished off the chicken pot pie quickly and was looking around for their waitress, probably interested in dessert.

Suzie came around and cleared their table. "Dessert for either of you?"

"I'll have a slice of that apple pie—the kind with the crumbs on top. Vanilla ice cream on the side, please. Anything for you, Gab?"

"Just another herbal tea, thanks."

After Suzie left to fill their order, Matt asked, "So, learn anything interesting from the file your friend in New York gave you?"

Gaby sat back, wondering how she should handle this. She paused for a few seconds, then said, "Not really." The weighty silence between them prompted her to add, "Turned out that the new approach to an advertising campaign Joe was trying out involved a US Senate race for a first-time candidate. Joe's work was halted before the ads could be created. I thought he might have uncovered something the candidate, Arnie Campbell, was afraid would cost him the election, leading to the termination of Joe's work on the campaign and to the attack that killed him."

"Really?"

"The people managing Campbell's campaign claimed they discontinued their work with Joe due to cost constraints, but I wondered, especially given that the stranger's note came now, when Campbell is running for reelection."

"And?"

"There was nothing in the file Carl gave me that even hinted at anything nefarious, and I'm sure Joe would have told me if there was. I ended up calling the people running his reelection campaign.

Turned out it's the same firm that helped Campbell get elected the first time around. Sounded like it really was a budget decision. The person I spoke with said they would have gladly hired Joe for the reelection campaign now that finances are less of a problem. I guess I believed him. In any event, there's nothing there, so I'll have to pursue other possibilities."

"Such as?"

"Not sure yet. Something in Joe's past maybe, but I doubt that. Still, something prompted the note."

"Ever think that you might have been the real target of the attack? That your husband just got in the way?"

Gaby stared silently at Matt, then shook her head. "I went down that blind alley back then. Nothing there."

"Mind if I look? It's what I'm trained to do," Matt said quietly. "Remember. My contacts with the NYPD helped you with that Lakeview Terrace thing."

"I know, but… can't you just leave this alone?"

"Nope. Not if you're in trouble, and I'm pretty sure you are." He paused. "By the way, I went up to the old Haverson place. The house is on the market. The lawn had been freshly cut, but no one was around. The real estate agent handling the property told me it had been purchased from the Haverson estate after Mrs. Haverson passed away. She never met the principal of the firm that handled the rehab on the house. Want me to continue sleuthing?"

"Matt? Please? Like I told you before, I just don't want you to be involved."

"Sorry, Gab. It's what I do… What I have to do. It's my job."

Gaby shook her head, her eyes smarting. She didn't want to cry in front of Matt and, instead, gulped down the rest of her tea, put her napkin on the table, and got up to leave.

"Good luck with the weekend. Let me know what I owe you for dinner," she said, making her escape out of the café and toward her car before her tears started falling.

Chapter 10

GABY GENTLY PUSHED THOUGHTS of Matt aside during her morning run the next day. She knew she shouldn't have left the café the way she had, without explaining why she didn't want Matt involved with the mystery concerning the stranger's note. She couldn't explain it to herself. It wasn't fair of her, and probably not wise, to push him away from protecting her from whatever danger he felt was awaiting her. He clearly wanted to help, but she just as clearly was saying, "No," and expected him to honor that, wise or not.

Back at her office desk after breakfast and a shower, Gaby reviewed the draft contract she had completed yesterday for a residential sale, then organized the remaining files based on her scheduled meetings with clients after the Fourth. Her calendar was packed for the days after the holiday next Tuesday, as well as the following week.

She retrieved the smaller of the piles of Pinkham's papers she'd sorted through yesterday, reflecting his personal correspondence, and brought these from the kitchen table back to her desk. She had inadvertently taken Pinkham's personal checkbooks—one for day-to-day expenses and the other for Sunrise Hills—when she scooped up the papers in his office and looked through both check registers and monthly statements to determine whether the seemingly unpaid bills she had found among these papers had actually been paid. They hadn't.

She decided to draft checks for the outstanding bills to bring to Pinkham for signature later in the week. She wanted to wait before visiting him again until she had some news to report on any success she might have in untangling land trust affairs from his own. Going through the pile of papers once again, she separated those related to the Sunrise Hills subdivision from Pinkham's personal correspondence and bills. It seemed he had been paying closer attention to expenses related to the subdivision than to his own.

She was wrapping up her work for the day when the phone rang. She glanced at the caller ID before picking up and didn't know whether she felt relieved or disappointed when she saw the caller wasn't Matt.

"Law offices, Gabriella Quinn speaking."

"Val Conway here, executive director and chief operating officer for the Woodson Falls Land Trust, Ms. Quinn. I understand you're assisting our Win Pinkham with his financial affairs, including those involving his volunteer work for the land trust. Under a valid power of attorney, I presume. Although I do not believe," he added, "it is appropriate for the reach of someone acting as a principal's agent to extend to managing aspects of an entity such as the WFLT."

"Excuse me?"

"Let me get down to it, Ms. Quinn. The land trust is poised to acquire a significant plot of land in the northern end of town. I've worked hard to convince the owner of the property to sell to the land trust rather than proceed with his plans to erect a senior affordable housing complex right on Woodson Falls' border with Prescott."

"Hmm… And?"

"I've been tracking donations made specifically toward this important acquisition, and my spreadsheet analysis reveals a significant drop-off in donations to save Meadow Ridge. The drop-off coincides exactly with the time our esteemed treasurer, Al Prunagle, had to move out of town suddenly and Pinkham picked up Al's duties as treasurer of the land trust. Never should have happened without my approval, of course. And old Win Pinkham should have resigned long before now. Really can't pull his own weight with the land trust, given his age and, well, you know."

"Know what?"

"Well, as I'm sure you've noticed, dear old Win's lost a few of his marbles along the way. More than a few, if you ask me. In any event, thank goodness he had the foresight to appoint someone to help him manage his affairs. Of course, regardless, those affairs shouldn't involve work for the land trust."

"Mr. Conway is it? I'm Mr. Pinkham's attorney, and while he has executed a durable power of attorney appointing me as his agent should he need assistance at some future date, he's as capable as you or me of managing his own affairs as well as those of the land trust," Gaby responded, shaking her head a bit at the pile of papers on her desk; the white lie she was telling on Pinkham's behalf, not the entire story. But Pinkham's mental capacity and his affairs certainly weren't hers to discuss with Conway. "Mr. Pinkham has long devoted time, energy and his own capital to the land trust, as I'm sure you're well aware, and deserves respect—and gratitude—for his efforts," she added.

Continuing, she said, "I'm sure there's a simple explanation for your observed fall-off in donations, but I'll have to check with Mr. Pinkham before discussing this any further with you. Why don't you give me your number so I can get back to you after I've had the chance to discuss this matter with him?"

Conway rattled off a number, then added, "I do hope you'll expedite your discussion with Pinkham. I need to have the information regarding the donations for the Meadow Ridge project soonest, along with any other land trust business that needs attending to."

"I'll see what I can do," Gaby responded, hoping she sounded non-committal—not wanting Conway to think she was following his directive. "Good day."

Gaby headed back to the kitchen to bring the pile of land trust papers to her office. She had hoped to leave them until after the holiday, but Conway's call prompted her to change her mind. She'd begin work on unraveling these issues first thing tomorrow. She didn't want to concede to Conway's allegations about Pinkham; instead, she hoped to provide a finished product Pinkham could submit to Hilda to acknowledge the donations, asking her to copy Conway on whatever she came up with.

The following morning, Gaby began by going through the pile of donations—loose checks, opened envelopes still containing checks, empty envelopes, completed donation forms—and separating these from other land trust documents. She hoped to follow Prunagle's spreadsheet approach to tracking donations to create an up-to-date record with respect to the trust for her client.

Gaby worked steadily through the day and into the evening, eating at her desk and only pausing long enough to attend to Kat's needs. She had pieced together most of the donations, even identifying the few deposits of land trust funds Pinkham had made to his personal account, which could be covered easily with a check of his own.

She'd have to deal later with the land trust checks that had been used to cover his subdivision expenses, which he'd also need to reimburse to the trust. No wonder Pinkham had gotten confused. The land trust checkbooks hidden among the papers she'd retrieved from his office were identical to his own, right down to the color of the covers and style and color of the checks.

It was after seven when she gave Pinkham a call. He answered after a single ring, and she recalled he had taken to carrying the portable phone in his pocket to save him the steps—and the effort—to retrieve it.

"Pinkham here."

"Hi, Mr. Pinkham… Win. Sorry, having trouble getting used to that," Gaby said with a chuckle. "It's Gaby. Sorry to be calling so late."

"Hello there. Not a problem, my dear. Always glad to hear from you. Just hope you aren't calling to tell me you're throwing in the towel in dealing with all those papers I left in a mess on my desk."

"Not at all. It's just that I got a call from a Mr. Val Conway—"

"Ah, the Exalted Leader and Grand Pooh-Bah of the WFLT, as Percival terms it," he answered with a chuckle. "You'd think he was managing a Fortune 500 company from the way he lords it over us 'little people.' Bet he told you I was senile and should have hung up my land trust hat years ago."

"Well, yes. He did suggest that. I thought he said his name was Val?"

"Hates Percival. That's why I use it." Pinkham's laugh was followed by a lengthy coughing fit.

"Are you okay?"

"Yes, I'm okay," he answered, his voice more gravelly than usual once he had caught his breath. "Hate the way he's managing the land trust, looking to merge with other small ones so he can rule a larger roost. I've talked with a number of my friends at the trust. They feel the same way. We all want it to stay small and more mean-ingful to Woodson Falls' residents than a larger organization might be. Would have 'hung up my hat' when he arrived, but didn't want to give him the pleasure. And I want to exert whatever influence I still have to keep the land trust a local operation."

"Good for you," Gaby laughed.

"He also has been working hard to try to convince me to abandon Sunrise Hills and donate the land to the trust outright or through my will, as I had originally planned. I've resisted those efforts, of course."

"Sounds like Conway."

"Any good news for me, my dear? I fear I've put you in the middle of a potential scandal."

"Not at all." Gaby told him what she'd been able to accomplish. "I'd like to meet with you tomorrow, if I could, to go over what I've done and plan with you how best to get those donations deposited and the list to Hilda so she can acknowledge them. Any time better for you?"

"Hmm… I have guests here right now. Friends from New York City. They arrived yesterday and will be staying with me until midday on Sunday. I'd rather put this off until after the holiday, if it's okay with you. Let Percy stew in his own juices."

Gaby laughed, "Sounds like a plan! Enjoy your guests. I'll give you a call after the Fourth."

Chapter 11

DESPITE THE WEATHER FORECASTER'S prediction of a cold and rainy holiday weekend, Sunday dawned with only the occasional puffy cloud in the pure blue sky. The cool breeze and mild temperature were perfect for the afternoon parade and evening fireworks display.

Gaby stopped at Mike's Place to pick up a sandwich and iced tea from a harried Emma Larson and headed to the village green to grab a good spot to watch the parade. She had spent the past two days unraveling Pinkham's financial affairs and felt she had gotten far enough for him to resume control of the situation. There were still some unanswered questions, but they could wait until she saw him later in the coming week.

Gaby was glad Pinkham had visitors for a few days. He seldom left his house, his accountant and bookkeeper seemingly the only people he saw regularly besides her, along with the woman who did his shopping and cleaning. The many beneficiaries named in his will suggested a fairly large circle of friends, but her client rarely spoke of them and most of their addresses were as far flung as those of his cousins.

Hauling her canvas chair from the trunk of her car, Gaby joined the rest of the crowd waiting for the show to begin. The sound of distant music eventually signaled the approach of the parade, which had begun farther north at the intersection of Meadow Ridge Road and Route 41. Gaby stood with the other observers as the honor guard of veterans passed by. The marchers paused across from Center Cemetery, the eerie trumpet notes of "Taps" bringing tears to Gaby's eyes. A veteran placed a wreath at the entrance to the cemetery. Like the small flags on the graves, the wreath would remain in place until Veterans Day, its bright flowers shriveled by then, their colors faded.

The parade resumed as the fire department vehicles passed, followed by the scouts. Someone had handed out small flags to the observers, and Gaby waved hers as vigorously as the others, clapping as each new group of marchers appeared. The Woodson Falls Elementary School band did a passable job with "I'm a Yankee Doodle Dandy," and she spotted Sally Gorman's son Ryan proudly beating his drum. Although he was a bit out of sync with the rest of the band, his big grin when he saw Gaby was a clear indication that he was enjoying himself.

Groups of marchers, some with floats, represented the various private communities in town. The crowd clapped in appreciation as a string of antique cars, a recent addition to the parade, followed the floats. Bringing up the rear was the Prescott High School marching band playing a medley of Armed Forces songs. The crowd's cheers accompanied the marchers as they gathered in groups across the green for the brief Independence Day ceremonies. Following the speeches, members of the parade committee would hand out bottles of water for the adults and ice cream cones for the children.

Despite the handheld microphone that was passed like a baton among the dignitaries arrayed around the portable podium, the speakers' voices could barely be heard, the breeze scattering their words across the lake. Still, the crowd watched attentively until the strains of the national anthem signaled the close of the event. The marchers dispersed, most joining the observers, who would be remaining in their seats for the fireworks display that would begin once the sun had set.

Ryan and his sister Ali ran up to Gaby. She occasionally stayed with the children while their mother, Sally Gorman, attended classes at the local community college. Sally's husband had been killed in the line of duty while serving in Afghanistan. Gaby had done her best to fill the deep hole the loss of their father had left for their children, seeing the family frequently and being especially attentive to the kids.

"Did ya see me, Mrs. Quinn? Did ya?" Ryan asked. It was the young boy's first year in the parade, and he was obviously proud of having marched with the school band.

"Sure did, Ryan. Great job there!" she replied, giving a hug to Ali, who was all decked out in her scout uniform. "Spotted you, too, Ali. You did a really good job holding up your end of the scout banner."

"Thanks," the young girl murmured, licking ice cream off her fingers.

"Mom said we could stay for the fireworks this year," Ryan said, taking his sister's hand. "We have to go find her."

"Off you go," Gaby said with a smile. "Enjoy!"

Leaving her chair where it was, Gaby got up to stretch and wandered among the crowd, chatting with people she knew. It was good to be out of the office and among others who lived in Woodson Falls. Though her law work kept her engaged with people, much of it was solitary. Like Pinkham, she was housebound a good deal of the time, despite her early morning runs and meetings with clients.

Heading back to her seat, Gaby spotted a young man in a Harvard sweatshirt standing not too far away who she recognized as Timothy Mitchell, son of the late writer, Phillip Mitchell, who had lived on Donovan's Way. The well-known writer had specialized in novels set during the French and Indian Wars. Gaby had worked with Tim in administering his father's estate.

"Tim!" she called, making her way through the crowd. "I thought you were planning to attend summer school."

"Gaby! Great to see you," he responded, giving her a hug. "After I read through Dad's early draft of his latest book, I was excited about picking up where he left off. I didn't want to lose my enthusiasm, so I decided to move into the cottage to write over the summer."

"You planning to return to Harvard in the fall?" Gaby asked.

"Sure," he responded, "but I felt so close to Dad reading the manuscript and didn't want to lose that sense of being connected to him. So far, the writing's going really well, and I'm pretty sure I'll be able to submit a draft of the book before I head back to Cambridge."

"Great news!" Gaby exclaimed. "Keep me posted. Maybe we can get together for dinner or something while you're still here in Woodson Falls."

"I'd love that," he answered, walking with her to her car. Then carrying the cooler she had retrieved from the trunk, he followed her back to her seat.

"My friend, Nell Whitney will be joining me in a bit." Gesturing to the cooler, she said, "Would you like to stay for some noshes before the fireworks begin? Nell's bringing beverages. I could give her a call to bring an extra soda or iced tea."

"Thanks, but no. I'm going to be heading back to Dad's place. Just took a break from writing to watch the parade."

"Well, good luck with the novel. I'll be in touch," Gaby said, giving the young man a parting hug. "So good to see you, and thanks for your help with the cooler."

After settling back in her seat, Gaby took in the view of the sparkling lake. Her thoughts turned to Matt. She was sure he was somewhere in the crowd, but she hadn't caught a glimpse of him.

Had she made a mistake in leaving the café so abruptly after their dinner together? Had she messed up this chance at a meaningful relationship? She wished she could go back in time and handle the whole situation differently. She really liked Matt, enjoyed his company, and was attracted to him. She hadn't felt this way about a man since Joe died. It seemed like it might be time to move on, but had she taken a giant step backward instead?

"Whew! What a day!" Nell exclaimed, interrupting Gaby's thoughts as she plunked down beside her friend in her own canvas chair. "Sold close to $2,000 worth of inventory! Haven't done that well in a long, long time!"

"Good for you," Gaby said, giving her friend a quick hug and taking the bottle of iced tea Nell held out for her. "Will you stay open on the Fourth?"

"Heavens, no! Not a good day for business. Most folks stay home and barbecue on the Fourth. Besides, Jackie and Ed are planning to come over with the kids. Would you like to join us?"

"Thanks," Gaby replied, "but no. I'm planning on vegging out. Need some 'me' time." She'd met Nell's daughter and grand-children, Susie and Robbie, though not Jackie's husband Ed. Her mind was filled with the stranger's note, Pinkham's problems, upcoming client meetings, and Matt. She didn't think she'd be good company. "Another time, perhaps."

"No problem," Nell answered, smearing a cracker with brie and popping a grape into her mouth. "How was the parade?"

Gaby laughed. "A few of the faces change from year to year, particularly the kids', but it's pretty much the same as always. Couldn't hear any of the speeches, but those were probably the same as well." She paused to take a swig of the iced tea. "Those antique cars they added surely were a hit."

"I'll bet," Nell responded. "There's something comforting about traditions that don't change much from year to year. But I don't think adding something to the parade every now and then takes away from that."

Gaby and Nell chatted amiably while the sun went down. As it got darker, the crowd settled, watching the boat from which the fireworks would be launched head slowly toward the center of Woodson Lake. Lake patrol boats were arrayed a good distance beyond it, poised to intercept any boaters who got too close to the action.

The fireworks display was spectacular, and the crowd "Oh'd" and "Ah'd," as usual. It was a fitting tribute to the birth of the nation. Like the parade, the constancy of the fireworks display was part of the comfort of living in a small town.

After packing up the near-empty cooler with empty bottles and folding their chairs, Nell and Gaby hugged, wished each other a happy Fourth, and made their way back toward their cars.

A loud boom and a sudden flare of fire over the distant hills stopped them both, as well as the rest of the crowd.

Gaby looked toward the plume of smoke rising in the north near the town's border with New York. "I warned Matt that there might be some residents shooting off fireworks," she said to Nell. "I wonder if a bunch were set off at once. I hope no one was hurt."

Nell shook her head. "Looks to me like a whole lot more than fireworks."

Chapter 12

The shrill ring of the phone greeted Gaby as she opened her cottage door upon returning from the Fourth of July festivities.

"Gaby, it's Matt," the caller announced before she could say hello. "Please don't hang up. There's been an accident."

"The explosion?" Gaby asked, hoping Matt was just ignoring her abrupt departure from the café and continuing their relationship as if it hadn't happened. "I heard it as I was leaving the town center. Anyone hurt?"

"Too early to tell," Matt responded. He paused. "That client you were telling me about the other day? You said his name's Winston Pinkham?"

"Yes?"

"He's at 2 Sunrise Trail?"

"Please don't say it was Win's house. Please say he got out and is okay. Please…" Gaby answered, her voice trembling.

"Sorry, Gab. That's the house, and there was no one outside when the fire department arrived." His last words were lost as Gaby dropped the phone and raced out of the cottage, calling to Kat to follow her.

Jumping into her car, Kat at her side, Gaby did her best to steady her hands and slow her breathing. Despite her rising panic, she drove carefully along the darkened roads. There were few street-lights in Woodson Falls, providing only the occasional puddle of light along the main roads. She made her way along Route 43, the most direct course to Pinkham's place from her own and one that avoided the likely tangle of cars leaving the town center after the fireworks.

Parking several yards down Route 43, her access to Sunrise Trail blocked by emergency vehicles, Gaby left her car tucked into the shoulder, clipped on Kat's leash, and ran toward Pinkham's road with Kat just ahead of her. A state trooper stopped her as she neared.

"Sorry, ma'am. This is an active scene. You can't be here. Please, just turn around and head back home or wherever you came from."

"But... but my client..." Gaby sputtered.

"It's okay, Jerry," Matt said, walking briskly toward Gaby and Kat. He gave the dog's head a scratch and added, "Ms. Quinn knows the owner of the house and may be able to help us in determining just what happened here."

"Your call, Matt. You're the lead officer," the trooper said, shaking his head, most likely wondering what help an obviously distraught woman and her dog, now leaning against the trooper's leg and wagging her tail vigorously, could possibly offer.

Matt took Gaby's elbow and guided her through the broad debris field, as close to the smoldering structure as the firefight-ing activity would allow. Several area fire departments, including the one from Prescott, had responded to the emergency. A maze of fire hoses lay on the ground around the house within a six-foot wide area that had been cleared of foliage, most likely to prevent the fire from spreading to the adjacent shrubbery and the forest beyond. Fire fighters close to the building were using hatchets to take down the few burning timbers that once supported walls. She thought she spotted Adam Samuelson among the men responding to the blaze, then doubted it was him. He just didn't seem to be the type to get involved in such a dangerous activity.

Except for the blackened planks, all that was left of the old wood-framed house was its stone foundation, the brick fireplace and its chimney, and half a wall. The air was thick on her tongue and burned her eyes. There weren't any visible flames. It looked like the efforts of the firefighters had controlled the burn. There really didn't seem to be anything left to feed the fire.

"Has anyone checked inside?" she asked, following Matt as close to the house as the continuing firefighting efforts and the heat radiating off the building allowed, a reluctant Kat trailing behind.

"The fire isn't completely controlled, even though you don't see flames. You can feel the heat from here, a good distance back. That smoldering wood could erupt into a blaze at any moment. The fire's been knocked down, but it still needs to be dampened to reduce the risk of recurrence. There'll be an investigation inside the building once it's safe to do so," he responded. "In the meantime, let me ask a few questions about your client."

"Okay," she said, her voice barely a whisper. Kat leaned into her, and Gaby stroked the dog's soft fur.

"Any idea where Pinkham might have been when the explosion occurred?"

"I'm afraid he'd be at home sitting in his armchair," she answered, continuing to stroke Kat's head. "I know he was expecting some guests over the past few days, but they were supposed to be leaving earlier today. They might have coaxed him out for a meal or two while they were visiting, but he rarely ventured out on his own. He'd given up driving quite a while back."

"You realize, Gaby, if he was in the house there's no chance he survived that blast," Matt said softly. "Is there family nearby? Do you know how to contact them?"

Gaby shook her head, her eyes brimming with tears that spilled down her cheeks. "Only two cousins, and they live far away. I'm probably the closest he has to family."

"I'm so very sorry," Matt said. "You said Pinkham was elderly. I know I asked you before, but what was his mental state?"

"He's totally competent," she answered sharply, his question reminiscent of the recent call from Val Conway. "Why?"

"You'd be surprised at how often a fire like this begins with a forgetful senior leaving a pot on the stove with the burner still on. Something in the kitchen—often a curtain or a dishtowel—catches fire and then it's off to the races."

"But the explosion. It had to be triggered by something more than an overheated pot."

"True. How did he heat the place? Oil furnace, electric, propane?"

"I'm not sure. I have his most recent bills and his checkbook and some banking statements, but I wasn't looking for that kind of information when I was going through them. Why? Is it important?"

"Gas leaks are the most common cause of house explosions. If he heated with propane or even just cooked with gas, either might explain the origin of the blast."

"If there was a gas leak, wouldn't he have smelled it? Recognized the odor and left the house?"

"Yes, if he didn't have mobility issues. But there was no one outside when the firefighters arrived. Anything else you can tell me?"

"He has lung disease and uses oxygen." Gaby was reluctant to speak of Pinkham in the past tense, although she was fairly certain he hadn't survived the blast. "But he used a concentrator, not a tank. Isn't an oxygen tank under pressure and more likely to explode than a concentrator, which just takes in air and pulls the oxygen from it?"

"That's true."

"And he smoked without turning off the concentrator when he lit up."

"Now there's a possibility! Actually, more a probability. If there was a gas leak, lighting a cigarette might trigger the explosion. Plus, his age and smoking habit might have diminished his sense of smell. He may not have noticed the odor of gas if that's what was the underlying cause of the explosion. Anything else?"

Gaby wiped her tears on the sleeve of her jacket. "I'm sorry. I just don't think I can do this now, Matt."

"I understand. In any event, the town's fire marshal will be investigating—that's him over there. He'll be calling in the state's Fire and Explosion Investigative Unit to go through the building with him. Can I give him your contact information? His name is Brian. Brian Mayfield."

"Sure," she said. "Thanks for letting me in to the scene. I needed to see for myself that it was Win's house, even though it's the only one on Sunrise Trail. At least, that's how I felt when you called. But now that I've seen this…" She paused, swallowing the sob threatening to interrupt her words. "It's just… It's just all so sad."

"I'm so very sorry, Gaby," Matt repeated, reaching out to draw her close in a hug but pulling back and only giving her shoulder a pat. "Let me walk you to your car."

"Hold up there, Officer," called the man Matt had identified as the fire marshal for Woodson Falls. "It's too soon to know for sure, but one of the firefighters thought he saw a body in there amid the ruins. Would you call Major Crimes and let them know what happened? It's unlikely that anything criminal occurred here. Just a tragic accident. But it'll be their call."

"Sure, Brian," Matt answered.

The fire marshal thanked him, then turned away, shaking his head. "Anyone inside that house when it blew up is sure to be one crispy critter."

Hearing him, Gaby burst into tears and ran back toward Route 43 and her car, followed closely by Kat.

Chapter 13

THE COLD AND RAIN predicted for the weekend arrived on Monday and persisted through the Tuesday holiday. Forced to stay indoors, Gaby found herself immobilized by a mixture of guilt and grief. Should she have been more insistent with Pinkham about the dangers of lighting his cigarettes while oxygen continued to flow from the nearby concentrator? Perhaps she could have prevented this tragedy, this probable death, which seemed to have hit her unusually hard. If only she hadn't bowed to his choice.

She knew the old man was fond of her and appreciated her visits. Should she have refused to come if he continued his incessant smoking? But that wasn't her. She valued personal autonomy. It wasn't her place to make decisions for her client. She had warned him of the dangers. It was his choice whether to heed her warning.

Dear Win had been like a grandfather to her, and his death had dredged up painful memories of other losses, beginning with her beloved grandmother and grandfather. She and her older sister Marcia had spent glorious summers with them here in Woodson Falls, in this very cottage Gaby had inherited from their grandfather when he passed away just a year after Gram. Being here brought with it memories of Marcia, who had died of meningitis while

Gaby enjoyed the whirl of college life in the city, too busy to travel up to the family home in Middletown, Connecticut, not knowing that she'd never have the chance to see her sister one last time. But the pain of these deaths paled when compared to the loss of her husband Joe, and the unbearable memory of his blood flowing across her as he lay dying in her arms after the stranger's attack.

Gaby shuddered, shook her head as if to chase those recollections away, and stood up from the kitchen table where she had been lingering over a cup of tea. She knew this was a dangerous road to travel, one that would only serve to pull her down into the depths of depression, once again trapped by grief.

She decided to busy herself with gathering the information needed for the application to probate Pinkham's will. In serving as his executor, she could, at the very least, honor his memory by fulfilling his final wishes as expressed in his will. Work would block this jumble of memory and regret. It might seep through when she was least aware of its lurking presence, but for now she could distract herself with action.

Gaby headed to her office, Kat trailing close behind, clearly attuned to the fragility of her owner's mood. Once there, she pulled out Winston Pinkham's bulky file. The original copy of his most recent will was on top. She smiled as she recalled her client's response when she offered him the option of retaining the original in his own files.

"What good would that do?" he had asked in his gravelly voice. "I'll be dead when it actually matters and, as my executor, you'd just have to go hunting for it. Better to leave it in your hands."

The original will had to be submitted to the probate court, along with a certified copy of the death certificate, before the court would entertain an application to probate the will and appoint the executor. It usually took about a week for a funeral home to issue the certificate. However, with the likelihood that Pinkham's body would be in the custody of the state's medical examiner, it might be some time before the official cause of death, most likely smoke inhalation and "thermal injuries," the euphemistic term for "burns," was entered on his death certificate.

It would take at least a few weeks for the body to be released for burial. Another requirement of the court was the submission of a paid funeral bill. Pinkham had expressed his wish to be cremated, with the remains consigned to the family's burial plot at Hope Cemetery in Barré, Vermont. Gaby shuddered as she wondered whether the remains likely to be recovered at Sunrise Trail would need to be subjected to a second round of fire.

Beyond the three essential documents—the will, death certificate and funeral bill—to be filed when initiating probate of an estate, Gaby would need to provide some basic information on the application. Most important were the names and addresses of each of the dozen beneficiaries identified in Pinkham's will. The names and addresses of any heirs—family members who had a legal interest in the estate, whether or not they were mentioned in the will—had to be listed as well. These could be found in his telephone book, which she had scooped up along with the other papers from Pinkham's desk. Gaby knew from her work with Pinkham that his only living relatives were two cousins, both of whom were named in the will, although their share in the estate was minimal, a mere $500 each. Most other beneficiaries would receive between five and fifteen percent of the entire estate.

The value of Pinkham's assets, other than that of the property at 2 Sunrise Trail and the property comprising the Sunrise Hills subdivision, had to be estimated on the application to probate the will. Gaby hoped to submit the required inventory reporting the value of each of the estate's assets, this time including the real estate, along with the application. She could access much of this information in the papers she had retrieved from Pinkham's office as well as through his accountant, whose name and contact information would be in Pinkham's telephone book.

Although she could determine the value of Pinkham's Sunrise Trail properties through the assessor's office, it might be wiser to have the land appraised by a specialist. In any event, much of this could be done while she was waiting for the medical examiner to do his work, issue the death certificate, and release what was left of Pinkham's body. Gaby made a list of calls she would make the next day.

She planned to call an appraiser she had used in the past to determine the value of the land at 2 Sunrise Trail as well as the lots laid out in the Sunrise Hills subdivision. Those values would be important in setting an asking price when she was able to sell the lots. That couldn't happen until the probate court formally appointed her as executor of the estate, at which time she'd engage a Realtor to handle the marketing of the lots.

When she was working with Pinkham to draft this latest version of his will, which referenced the subdivision, she knew this would be a complicated estate to administer. She had hoped the whole subdivision project would be completed and the lots sold before she had to take over his affairs, but that was not to be.

While he had discussed with Gaby the idea of creating a codicil to his will, leaving the Sunrise Hills property to the Woodson Falls Land Trust if he died before the road was put in and the lots sold, he hadn't acted on the thought. Of course, such a codicil would have left Adam and Bud without a bequest from Pinkham, but then she wouldn't have to deal with those two men, which would have been a relief.

Gaby would need to contact Pinkham's accountant, both to notify him of the likelihood of Pinkham's death and to request a statement indicating the date of death values of his investment holdings. She also wanted to know the value of his charitable remainder trust, which had been drafted by another attorney long before she began her law practice in Woodson Falls. The trust had been making periodic payments to Pinkham, with the remainder to be donated to the Woodson Falls Land Trust upon his death. Although this asset wasn't subject to probate, it still had to be reported to the court.

She knew Percival Conway would be pestering her about the "missing" donations to the land trust. He'd be pleased to hear that she had the checks in hand as well as the news about the trust, but she didn't want to let him know of its existence until she knew its value and was certain it was Pinkham who had died in the explosion.

When the medical examiner was ready to release Pinkham's remains, she planned to ask that these be sent to the Wallace Funeral Home in Prescott. She had used them to handle Jorgenson's remains following the case at 16 Lakeview Terrace after learning that transferring remains to another state had to be done through funeral homes. While it wasn't true for cremains, it would be easier to make those arrangements with the people at Wallace, who could transfer the remains to the funeral home in Barré, Vermont, for internment there. She wondered who she would need to contact to ensure the medical examiner's office worked with her on the disposition of Pinkham's remains.

She was sure she'd hear from the fire marshal, Brian Mayfield, or possibly Matt, when the cause of Pinkham's likely death had been established and his remains were ready for release. She'd wait to hear from one or the other of them.

Then there was the insurance on Pinkham's house to be claimed. She could contact that company for the necessary paperwork while waiting for copies of his death certificate to be issued.

She certainly had more than enough to keep her occupied over the next week or two and hoped the work would keep her thoughts from straying to a dark place.

Chapter 14

THE MISERABLE WEATHER that had ruined backyard Fourth of July celebrations cleared overnight, and Wednesday began with a bright sun in a cloudless sky. Mist was rising from the soaked ground as Gaby took an early morning run with Kat. She had a full day ahead, as well as a busy schedule for the rest of the holiday-shortened week, including tackling the many calls she would be making in relation to Pinkham's estate. More than enough to keep her mind occupied and her emotions at bay.

The phone was ringing as she returned to the cottage short of breath. It was 7:45 in the morning. Who could be calling so early? Perhaps a client with a last-minute cancellation? That would free up her jam-packed day a bit.

"Law offices," she answered, "Gabriella Quinn speaking."

"Sorry to be calling so early, Ms. Quinn. Conway here. Val Conway. With the land trust?"

"Good morning, Mr. Conway. How can I help you?" Gaby hoped her voice didn't communicate the scowl on her face, not because of the early hour, but rather, the possible disrespect for Pinkham's passing Conway's call signaled to her. She was certain both the explosion and the identity of the house's owner had been reported widely, along with the news that a body had been spotted in the rubble.

"I read in the morning paper that Win Pinkham's house burned to the ground over the weekend. Do you know if he was the victim mentioned in the news?"

"The authorities believe there's a body in the house, but the remains have not been recovered and so haven't been identified to the best of my knowledge," Gaby said. "Mr. Pinkham seldom left the house, so I have to assume he was killed in the explosion. The house itself is a total loss."

"What a tragedy!" Conway replied, then hurriedly added, "No chance any paperwork related to the land trust could be recovered?"

"Everything in the house is gone, of course." Gaby answered, already prepared to tell another white lie. "However, I spoke with Mr. Pinkham following your previous call and he asked me to pick up the donations that had come in after the land trust treasurer's departure as well as the information on the donors Mr. Pinkham had prepared for the land trust secretary who handles the acknowledgments. As I'm sure you are aware, Mr. Pinkham seldom left the house. He asked me to deposit the donations and to transfer the donor information to a spreadsheet, similar to the treasurer's report. He doesn't—didn't have a computer, hence his request to me."

"Well, then." Conway's sigh of relief was audible.

"Anything else? I have a busy day ahead," Gaby said, eager to get off the phone.

"If you don't mind. Did he leave anything to the land trust in his will?"

"You'll have to wait a bit on that information. As I said earlier, although it's most likely that Mr. Pinkham died as a result of the explosion, the body spotted in the ruins of the house has yet to be confirmed as his. It'd be premature to discuss his estate at this time."

"Of course, of course. Well, it's a relief to know that the donations to save Meadow Ridge are intact. That's a really important acquisition for WFLT to add to its holdings. Can you send me a copy of the donor information when you send it off to Hilda Morrow, the land trust's secretary?"

"Why don't you ask Ms. Morrow for a copy, Mr. Conway? I'll get the spreadsheet off to her later today if I have the time."

"Humph! Well, then. Have a good day, Ms. Quinn," a clearly miffed Conway said, ending the call before Gaby could say goodbye.

"And good day to you, and good riddance," Gaby mumbled as she set about making a pot of coffee to have with her breakfast. She showered, then changed into slacks and a simple top to wear to her many appointments. The phone rang again as she poured her breakfast cereal.

"Law offices," she answered.

"It's me, Gaby," said Nell at the other end of the line. "Just read about the explosion and fire at 2 Sunrise Trail. Is that what we saw Sunday night?"

"Yes, I'm afraid it is. The house belonged to a longtime client of mine, Winston Pinkham. A body was seen in the wreckage. I'm assuming it's his, though that still has to be confirmed by the medical examiner. It's just a blessing there weren't any other homes in the area. They would have burned as well."

"Oh, dear!" Nell exclaimed. "How are you holding up?"

"It's hit me hard. Win was like a second grandfather to me. Now I have to manage his estate. He had no close relatives and named me as his executor."

"That's got to be difficult on many levels. Wasn't he involved in developing a piece of property?"

"Yes, and that complicates matters significantly. The planning and zoning commission finally approved the subdivision plans, and Win paid the road bond so the lots could be sold. Now I'll have to engage a contractor to do the road and drainage work as well as a real estate agent to sell the properties after I have each lot appraised. Lots more work than a run-of-the-mill estate."

"Indeed! I'm wondering if you'd be able to fit in lunch this Monday, perhaps in Prescott at the Greene Bean. My treat."

"That would be delightful. Let me see if I can clear my schedule," Gaby answered, then paused. "I've been feeling so alone lately. Win's death stirred up a lot of memories of past losses. And I had a falling out of sorts with Matt. It would be so good to talk with you. By that time, I may know a bit more about what might have caused the explosion on Sunrise Trail and whether it was, indeed, Win who died."

"Not good to keep all that pent up inside. Give me a call or stop by the shop to let me know if you're free on Monday."

The friends said goodbye and, checking the clock, Gaby sat down to enjoy her breakfast and a cup of coffee before heading out to see her clients.

After visits with three clients in the morning, all residents of Woodson Falls, Gaby stopped for a quick lunch at the Sunshine Café before heading to Prescott for a real estate closing scheduled for three o'clock at the Village Savings Bank. She hoped to stop in at the Prescott Town Hall first to get information for the quitclaim deed she would be drafting for another client.

She had just given her order to the waitress when her cell phone rang. Only a few people had her number, given the spotty service throughout Woodson Falls, but she didn't recognize the caller.

"Gaby Quinn," she answered.

"Ms. Quinn, this is Brian Mayfield, the fire marshal for Woodson Falls. Officer Thomas gave me your number. Am I calling at a bad time?"

"No, not at all. Just stopped for a bite of lunch between appointments. How can I help you?"

"Officer Thomas thought you might be able to provide some information about the owner of the house that blew up on the Fourth. Said he was your client?"

"Yes. His name is—was Winston Pinkham. I'm assuming he died in the fire."

"Any chance you might meet with me later today to go over a few things—fill in a few blanks?"

"I'll be tied up in Prescott until 4:00 or 4:30 this afternoon, but I could meet with you when I'm back in Woodson Falls. The rest of my week is filled with appointments."

"I sure would like to see you today, if at all possible. Could I save you a trip into town and meet you at your place at around five? I'll wait if you are delayed returning from Prescott. I need to submit a report to the State's Fire and Explosion Investigation Unit. They've been pressing me for the information, but with the holiday and such…"

"Of course. I'm at 6 Beaver Trail, off Pine Hill Road. South end of town."

"Thank you, Ms. Quinn. I'll see you then."

As the call ended and her meal arrived, Gaby wondered how she could frame the information she had in a way that wouldn't damage Pinkham's reputation or her own. She still felt vaguely guilty that she had tolerated Win's smoking habit and not made more of a fuss over the dangers of smoking with the oxygen flowing from the cannula dangling around his neck.

Chapter 15

ARRIVING HOME after a long day of work, pleased with all she was able to accomplish, Gaby let Kat out the door and brought her stuffed briefcase into her office. She knew the day's various meetings had generated work that would have to be tackled over the next week, but she was happy to have moved forward on the cases represented by the files that had been piled on her desk.

Taking time to freshen up, she filled Kat's water bowl and had just let the dog back in when the man she recognized as the fire marshal came strolling up the flagstone walkway.

"Mr. Mayfield?" Gaby asked.

"That'd be me," Mayfield said, shaking Gaby's proffered hand and following her into the cottage. "Thanks so much for seeing me on such short notice."

"No problem. Can I offer you iced tea, lemonade, something else?" Gaby asked, leading him to the den.

"Thanks, but no. I don't want to take up any more of your time than necessary," he responded, a weary smile on his face. Middle-aged and of middle height, Mayfield's round face was topped by fading blond hair. He sank into the leather chair next to the fireplace and pulled a small notebook from his shirt pocket, along with the stub of a pencil.

Kat had joined Gaby when she answered the door and followed the two into the den, lying on the floor next to Gaby as she settled herself on the sofa. "How can I help you?"

"Matt—Officer Thomas said you knew the owner of the house on Sunrise Trail. Thought you were the person who knew most about him."

"He's been—was—a longtime client. Lots of friends, a few distant relatives, most far from Woodson Falls. I was fond of him."

"Our investigation did reveal a body in the wreckage. Thomas said you were pretty sure it was the owner, Winston Pinkham?"

"I'm afraid it's most likely. He seldom left the house. Didn't drive. He told me some friends from New York were visiting for a few days, but they were leaving late Sunday morning. So, yes, I'm pretty sure it was dear old Mr. Pinkham who died in the explosion."

"Burn victims are hard to identify. In a case like this, dental records often are the best means of identification. Has the medical examiner called you? Asked you about Pinkham's doctor, dentist? I gave him your contact information. Told him he should treat you as he would next of kin based on what Officer Thomas told me. I hope you don't mind."

"Not at all. I am—was—closer to him than any of his few family members, so I appreciate that. Really, anything I can do to help. I haven't had the chance to check my phone messages yet. He may have already called, in which case I'll call him back when we're finished here."

Settling deeper into the chair, Mayfield took a deep breath before saying, "I know you told Officer Thomas about your client smoking while oxygen was flowing and that he used a concentrator rather than a tank. Can you verify that?"

"I begged Mr. Pinkham to turn off the oxygen concentrator when he felt the need to smoke, but he would just smile and ignore me. He'd been smoking for years and now that he'd reached his late eighties, I knew he'd be unlikely to break the habit. But I was concerned about the danger—the risk he was taking each time he lit up with the nasal cannula around his neck, oxygen flowing through it." Gaby shook her head before continuing. "Still, he'd been doing that forever and nothing had happened."

"You'd be surprised at how often we run into the same thing. Do you have any idea why he was receiving oxygen?"

"Chronic obstructive pulmonary disease—COPD—I think the doctor said when I took him to one of his appointments," Gaby ventured. "Probably as a result of his long history of smoking."

"Yeah," Mayfield responded. "I had an uncle with the same diagnosis—and the same cause. He was on oxygen through a concentrator, much like your Mr. Pinkham. Any idea what level of oxygen he was receiving?"

"I believe the concentrator was set at two percent, but his pulmonologist would be the one to check that with. Why do you ask?"

"It's usually between two and four percent for COPD. We'll check, of course, but…" Mayfield paused as if unsure whether he should continue. "We found the concentrator valve locked at ten percent oxygen. Those machines lock themselves when the flow is interrupted for any reason. Any chance Pinkham fiddled with the controls?"

"No chance of that. He may not have paid attention to the smoking issue and the danger posed by lighting up with oxygen flowing, but he was meticulous in other aspects of his life."

"Okay. Needed to ask. It's one of the anomalies we'll have to follow up on." Mayfield jotted something in his notebook.

"There are others?" When the fire marshal didn't respond but instead looked out the window, Gaby continued, "Were you able to learn anything else at the house? I guess the fire destroyed any evidence you might have found about what caused the explosion."

"Ve haf our vays," he said with a chuckle, his imitation of Colonel Klink from the old sitcom not far off. "Seriously, though, there are markers in every case. Often it's a matter of what *isn't* there that can be as important as what *is*. For example, there was no evidence of an accelerant—other than the oxygen—that might have supported the fire that followed the explosion."

"Matt—Officer Thomas asked me whether Win might have used propane for cooking or, possibly, to heat his house. Said a propane leak was the most common cause of a house explosion. I have access to his most current bills and past expenditures—"

Mayfield looked at her with one eyebrow raised, and Gaby wondered if yet another person was questioning Pinkham's competence, particularly in light of his question concerning the concentrator valve.

"Long story. He had mixed up his personal financial affairs with those of the land trust he does volunteer work for. There was a lot going on… Anyway, I checked and he did use propane to heat his home as well as to cook. I think he had converted his fireplace from wood-burning to propane as well. Does that information help?"

"Very much so," Mayfield responded, putting away his notebook and pencil.

"Can I ask you something else?"

"Sure," Mayfield answered, hands on his knees.

"I know that the victim's body was sent to the medical examiner."

"Always happens in a case like this."

"Any idea when he might complete his work? Release the body? I'll have to make arrangements if it's Mr. Pinkham who died."

"You'll be able to get something more definitive from him when you talk with him, but it usually takes a few days unless something unusual is uncovered. They'll be in touch with you concerning the disposition of the body once it's been identified. And they'll need contact information for any next of kin. They always inform the relatives of the deceased—even distant ones—before releasing any information to the public."

Mayfield stood. "Thanks again for making time for me."

Gaby led the fire marshal to the front door. "Please let me know if there's anything else you need."

"I will, and I'll let you know if we learn anything more about just what happened that night."

"Thanks. I'd appreciate that."

Mayfield started down the walkway, then turned to look back at Gaby. "I realize my remark at the fire scene—my reference to 'crispy critters'—upset you. I'm really sorry about that. Gallows humor. Helps us get through some of the horrors we encounter in this work, but I really need to put a lid on it when I'm around others. I'm truly sorry for upsetting you."

"Thank you for that," Gaby said, slowly closing the door as Mayfield continued toward his car, tears in her eyes as she recalled the ruins of Pinkham's home, convinced he had perished in whatever had happened to cause the disaster and hoping he hadn't suffered.

Chapter 16

Nell was sitting on the bench outside the Greene Bean, enjoying the beautiful summer day, when Gaby approached the storefront eatery. Most Prescott restaurants were closed on Mondays, and the small patio next to the Greene Bean was crowded.

"Guess we'll have to sit inside," Gaby said, giving her friend a hug. "If there's even room in there."

"I asked Judy to save a table for us," Nell said, getting up. The friends made their way into the small restaurant. Once seated, they picked up their menus to make their choices before a waitress came to their table.

"Drinks, ladies?" asked the young woman, clearly harried with so many guests to serve.

"I'll have the hibiscus lemon iced tea," answered Nell.

"And I'll have the peppermint, please," Gaby said, "along with…" But their waitress had whisked away to get their beverages, not waiting for the rest of their order. It would be a long lunch, Gaby suspected, but that was okay. The friends had lots of ground to cover.

"So," Nell began, "any progress on the Sunrise Trail matter?"

"Some," Gaby answered, fiddling with her silverware. "I had a call from the medical examiner's office. They had asked how to reach Win's dentist and, based on the dental records, they were able to positively identify the body as Pinkham's. No cause of death yet, so no death certificate, meaning I'm not able to initiate probate of his estate. Said there were 'anomalies' to be explored further, but declined to give me anything more."

"That has to be unsettling," Nell said, looking up as their drinks arrived, ready to order, but their waitress had been flagged at another table. "Ah well, soon enough I suppose." Whether she was referring to having their order taken or Gaby being able to start her work on Pinkham's estate was unclear.

Gaby smiled. "Very unsettling, but there's enough preliminary work to get me started. I've got an appraiser coming out tomorrow to value the real property and suggest what the lots might be sold for. I have to hold off on contacting a company to clear the debris left by the explosion. The fire marshal also said there were some irregularities that had to be analyzed further before he could give me an all clear to proceed on that front. And of course, I can't claim the house insurance until I have Win's death certificate in hand and I'm appointed executor."

"That's odd. Didn't you tell me your client smoked while receiving oxygen therapy? Wasn't that the likely cause of the explosion?"

"Apparently not, but I don't really know." Gaby brushed a tear from her cheek. "I'm just so sad. I feel stuck not knowing what actually happened, and I feel guilty about not being more insistent about his smoking with the oxygen flowing. I know that's silly of me, but without being able to move ahead on the formalities involved with the probate of his estate in any meaningful way, I feel like I'm sitting on my hands, not accomplishing anything. Though heaven knows, I've got enough going on with my law practice to divert my attention."

"I'm so sorry," Nell said, patting her hand. "This all has to be so hard for you."

The awkward moment was interrupted by their waitress's appearance. "Ready to order, ladies?" she asked.

"I'll have the Caesar salad with grilled chicken, dressing on the side, please," Gaby said.

"And I'll have the Cuban wrap, please, along with a serving of fries," Nell answered, turning to Gaby. "Which we'll share."

"Got it. I'll refill your iced teas as soon as I have a minute. It's crazy here today," she said, heading toward the kitchen only to be waylaid by another diner.

"Change of subject," Gaby said. "What's going on with you?"

"Hold on there. Something else is bothering you about the whole Win Pinkham matter."

"You know me too well," Gaby said with a small smile. "Too many people I've encountered in all this have questioned Win's competence, but I didn't see any signs of diminished capacity. Makes me angry and yet…"

"And yet you're wondering if you might have missed something. And whether that 'something' might be significant."

"I've been Win's attorney for years. He was one of my first clients when I opened my practice in Woodson Falls. Maybe I didn't see the signs he was failing mentally."

"It's easy to miss with someone you're close to. In a way, I think we fill in their blanks and assume all is well."

"Could be. He really made a tangle of handling his personal finances, transactions related to the subdivision, and then the land trust stuff on top of it. Yet he'd had a banking career, and I guess I assumed he was just overwhelmed, especially considering the delays with the Sunrise Hills project."

"Anything's possible, but that's moot now, isn't it?"

"Yes. I need to forget about that as well as his smoking with the oxygen running. Can't go back in time to undo any of it." Gaby shook her head as if to chase those thoughts away. "So now, what's new with you? How did the Fourth go with Jackie and her family?"

"Okay, I guess, given the rain we had that day. Hard to have a barbecue when you can't be outside! Jackie's husband, Ed, was a real sport! Put on rain gear and manned the grill while Jackie and I stayed inside and prepared the sides. The kids were content to watch a movie on TV. But it's just not the same indoors as out."

"It *was* a gloomy Fourth, and I'm super-glad I had already decided not to drive up to Massachusetts to see Joe's family. Staying home was my better bet, even with how low I was feeling.

"I'm just glad the parade and fireworks went off without a hitch! I know the parade committee will have folks march rain or shine, but it's a lot more fun when it's sunny."

The waitress brought their meals. "Anything else I can get you, ladies?" she asked.

Nell looked at Gaby, who shook her head. "Just another iced tea for each of us. Otherwise, I think we're fine, thank you."

They ate for a bit, then Nell said with a big smile, "We may have a new store in town!"

"Where? There's no room in the center as it is with all the town's stores in one place. Is someone leaving? Oh, not Frank, I hope. I'd be lost without the gadgets he carries in his hardware store as well as his do-it-yourself advice."

"No, it's the store next to mine! The hair salon. Nancy Beachum says she's ready to retire. Heading to Florida sometime after Thanksgiving! She's undergone two work-related carpal tunnel surgeries in the last couple of years and says she's had enough. She has a loyal following, both in Woodson Falls and southern Prescott. There'll be a lot of disappointed clients when she closes shop!"

"Is she selling the business to another hairdresser?"

"Doesn't want to go to the effort. She plans to sell her equipment and be finished with it."

"I wonder what will end up in that space. It's tricky to find a business that can survive, never mind thrive, in a small town like Woodson Falls."

"Someone's already making inquiries. New person in town."

"Really? What kind of store do they want to open?"

"A bookstore!"

"A bookstore?"

"Yes! Delightful woman, a bit quirky, but I think you'd like her. Her name's Myra Nichols. She and her husband bought that old brick house on Shadow Lane and are rehabbing it."

"That's gotta be a lot of work—and a lot of money. The few times I've passed there, I wondered when it was going to cave in."

"Well, I guess the bucks are there. Her husband manages a hedge fund. Something to do with cryptocurrency, I think. Travels a lot. The house project is Myra's. Says planning the rehab and finding the right workers kept her busy when they first moved up here from the city. But with her husband away a good deal of the time, she doesn't want to be stuck hanging around while the place is being worked on. She's been looking for something to occupy her time. Says she's always dreamed of owning a bookstore, and Nancy leaving opened up the opportunity."

"But a bookstore? In Woodson Falls? Do you think that has any chance of succeeding?"

"Who knows? Time will tell. Who would have thought a place selling herbs and crystals would survive for all the years I've owned Rainbows & Unicorns?"

"True. But wouldn't a bookstore cut into your own business? You carry a lot of books, even though you're not really a bookstore. Still, they're tucked here and there along with the candles and stones and teas. And that section of books by local authors…"

"Myra and I talked about that. We think we could work it out so there's no overlap. Even find a way to complement one another, like a children's book section in her store, with a focus on unicorns and rainbows. And I could refer people interested in gemology or growing herbs to seek a reference book from Myra's place. Who knows? Might work! And there's no reason we can't both carry local authors' books. After all, it's more exposure for the authors!"

"A bookstore. Well, now I've heard everything! More power to her," Gaby said, shaking her head. "But here's a thought. Remember back when I was just getting involved with the Donovan's Way case and picked your brain about Phillip Mitchell, the local author who wrote novels set in the French and Indian Wars?"

"Yes?"

"Mitchell's son, Timothy, was hoping to pick up where his father left off with the book he was working on. Tim traveled with his dad on a field trip to gather information for the book, so he has a good grasp of the material. Mitchell's publisher jumped at the idea."

"And?"

"Tim's a student at Harvard. He'd been planning to take courses during the summer session so he could take a leave of absence during the fall semester to complete the novel. I talked with him at the parade. He was so eager to begin working on the book he decided instead to move into the cottage on Donovan's Way and work on the book over the summer. Hopes to have a first draft off to the publisher by the time he heads back to Harvard to continue his studies. If the timing is right, maybe Tim could do a reading and sign copies of the book at our new bookstore!"

"That would be sweet. Really get Myra off to a solid start! And if her dream of a bookstore in Woodson Falls doesn't material-ize, I could invite Tim as a guest author at Rainbows & Unicorns.

"But enough! What's going on with Matt?"

Chapter 17

"It all started with the note."

"What note?" Nell asked, munching on a french fry.

"Oh my!" Gaby exclaimed. "I never told you about the note?"

Nell shook her head. "I don't think so. Was it from Matt?"

"Goodness no! With everything that's been going on, I guess I just buried it and its implications in a far recess of my mind."

Nell sat back. "Time to explain, girlfriend."

"Two, three weeks ago, I was having breakfast at the café. Helen gave me an envelope, saying someone I had seen at the counter way back in March—at the start of the Lakeview Terrace case—had left it for me recently. The envelope contained a curt note warning me not to 'go down the same path as Joe,' or something like that."

"You're kidding!" Nell exclaimed, then seeing Gaby's expression, said, "You're *not* kidding."

"No, not kidding." Gaby picked a crouton out of the salad she'd been nibbling at and popped it into her mouth.

"Why didn't you tell me?"

"I assumed you'd suggest I forget it, which is what Helen said to do. And I just didn't feel I could."

"Hmm… I'm not sure what I would have said, but go on."

"I didn't know what to do at first, but then I decided to call an old friend Joe worked with at the ad agency, Carl Grant. I thought the note might refer to something Joe was involved with at work. I knew it was a stretch. He's been dead, what, six years? But it was a start."

"Okay. Putting that to one side for now, how is all this related to whatever's going on with Matt?"

"Helen told Matt that, after I read the note she had given me, I ran out of the café without touching the pancakes I'd ordered. Matt called to ask what the note said and wanting to help. I told him I needed to work it out for myself."

"But he's trained in that sort of thing. Why wouldn't you welcome his help?"

Looking up at Nell, Gaby said, "That's what Matt wanted to know." She took a swallow of her diluted tea. The ice cubes had melted a while back, and their waitress hadn't refreshed their drinks as promised. "I really, really loved Joe. And when he died, I felt like my heart died with him. That I hadn't just lost *him*, but also the capacity to love anyone else in the same way, ever." She went to take another sip of tea, but abandoned the effort, setting the glass aside. "But I really, really like Matt. I feel differently about him than I have about any other man I've met since I lost Joe. I just didn't want… I don't know how to say this."

"You didn't want your past to collide with a possible future?"

"How do you do that?"

"Do what?"

"Put into words what I'm feeling—better than I can express it myself."

Nell smiled. "I didn't exactly live under a rock after David and I divorced."

"But this is different."

"Not really. But go on. You said you had a falling out with Matt somewhere along the line?"

Gaby sighed. "I finally showed Matt the note and told him I would ask for his help if I needed it, and we left it at that. Then…"

Their waitress finally arrived to pick up their empty plates. "So sorry for the delays. I'll bring you fresh iced teas right away. Any dessert for either of you?"

"An oatmeal chocolate chip cookie," Nell and Gaby said in unison.

"Two cookie specials, coming up."

"You were saying…" Nell prompted.

"Then, just before the Fourth, Matt called to ask if I'd join him for dinner at the café. Said he had some questions about the holiday in Woodson Falls, what he should be on the lookout for. But he really just wanted some company.

"I was getting cross-eyed working on Pinkham's finances when he called and was wondering what I would do about dinner, so I met him at the café. Everything went along fine. He's just so easy to be with. But then he started up again about the note. Said he thought it might be directed at me. That I might have been the original target of the attack. I told him I'd been over all that back then and explained again that I didn't want him involved, but he kept pushing. So…"

"Sorry again for the delays," their waitress said, putting down their fresh iced teas and offering each a cookie on a plate. "Cookies are on the house, Judy says."

"Well, thank you." Nell looked around the restaurant and gave a wave to Judy, who was at the register. "So then?"

"I walked out."

"You walked out? Without saying anything? Just left?"

"Afraid so. I was angry with him for not listening to what I was saying about not wanting him involved. And… and I didn't want to cry in front of him."

"Hmm… Have you seen Matt since then?"

"He called me the night of the explosion. He was checking to see if it was my client's house that had blown up. I had told him a little about Win. I headed right over to Sunrise Trail and Matt let me into the scene. We talked a bit about Win and the possible causes of the explosion. Something the fire marshal said upset me and I nearly broke down, so I rushed away from Sunrise Trail. I did tell Matt how much I appreciated his letting me see what had happened, but our focus was on what we were looking at and what might have caused it, not on us."

"Have you heard from him since?"

"No. I had hoped I'd run into him, but honestly, I don't even know what I'd say."

They paused and each took a big bite of cookie, the warm chocolate dripping on their fingers, which they licked.

"Tell me," Nell said. "Deep down, how do you feel about Matt? I mean, beyond 'really, really' liking him."

Gaby smiled. "It's so confusing. After Joe and I were married, I used to think what a joy it was to no longer be searching for that special someone to share my life with. And after he was killed, I couldn't imagine reengaging with a man in that way."

Nell cocked her eyebrow in a question.

"You know. The boy-girl stuff. Flirting."

"You mean sexually?

"I guess. Yes." Gaby took a deep breath. "When I first met Matt, at the police station here in Prescott no less, something long dead in me came alive again. There was a spark. I thought it was just those incredible blue eyes of his, but when he rescued me later that night after I had been run off the road, I found it so easy to talk with him. I was shook up from the accident, of course, but I felt so comfortable being with him. Each time I see him, I still feel that way.

"When I finally broke down and told him what had happened to Joe, back when we were working on the stuff at Donovan's Way, he hugged me. I still can recall so vividly the feel of his arms around me, even now. I know that a successful relationship involves more than sexual intimacy, but I feel that spark of physical attraction when I'm with Matt, and somehow I think he feels that too. But it's more than that. I feel like we could have a comfortable companionship."

Gaby laughed to herself. "Problem is, I'm out of practice. It's like a dance I've forgotten how to do. And I really believe I ruined any chance I might have had with him when I walked out of the café and left him there."

"I would doubt that. Neither of you is a kid anymore, holding on to petty grudges. You're both in a different place. Didn't you tell me that, like you, he had been married and widowed? You each bring all that past—the good and the not-so-good—to your relationship. I suspect you'll find a way to connect again. Maybe not right away, but it'll happen."

"You're a hopeless romantic if you think that," Gaby said with a sad smile. "Nice thought, but I'm sure I really pushed him away without intending to."

"We'll see," Nell said, picking up the check.

Gaby grabbed her purse and said, "What do I owe you?"

"My treat, remember? I'm so glad we got together. And I'm so glad you felt comfortable enough to share your feelings about Matt with me." She patted Gaby's hand. "It'll work out, one way or the other. Just give it time."

"Thanks for lunch," Gaby said, giving Nell a long hug as they both stood to leave. "You're such a good friend."

Driving back to Woodson Falls, Gaby thought again how lucky she was to have met Nell. What a true friend she was. Getting out of the car, Gaby heard Kat barking. It wasn't her greeting bark. Something had disturbed her.

Nearing the cottage, Gaby noticed something on her door fluttering in the breeze as well as a dark shape on the doorstep. As she got closer, she recognized the fluttering as coming from a note pinned to the door.

I know where you live. Watch your step.

Looking down, Gaby paled as she saw a nearly decapitated, scrawny black cat laid out on the stone step in front of her door.

Chapter 18

GABY'S RECENT EXPERIENCES with crime scenes had taught her not to do anything that would disturb whatever evidence might be associated with the note and the dead cat. But she could hear Kat frantically scratching at the door and barking. She wanted to get her dog out of the house before setting off to find Matt. She knew she wouldn't have cell service here on Beaver Trail, but when she considered going into her house to use a landline, her heart began racing and her body tensed.

Going around to the back door, which opened into her kitchen, she unlocked it and whistled for Kat to come. Careful not to step into the house, she reached around the door to grab Kat's leash from the doorknob where it was hanging and clipped it to her collar as soon as the dog appeared in the doorway. She didn't want to risk having Kat run to investigate the dead animal.

Coaxing a whimpering Kat into the car, Gaby made her way toward town, hoping that Matt was in his office. His cruiser was parked outside the fire department, signaling his presence. She pulled into the space beside him.

With Kat on a leash, she went into the building and knocked gently on the door to the trooper's office. He opened it, phone to his ear, and beckoned her in, pointing to the chair in front of his desk.

Ending his phone call, Matt sat opposite her and leaned back in his chair, looking at Gaby. "So, to what do I owe this pleasure?"

Gaby colored slightly, recalling her recent chat with Nell, then said, "I need your help."

Matt raised his eyebrows. "If it's about what went on at 2 Sunrise Trail, I haven't heard anything yet."

"No, it's not that." She took a deep breath and then blurted, "I think you might be right. I think I might be in danger. Someone was at my cottage. They left a note—the handwriting looks the same as the one I got at the café. And there's a dead cat lying on my doorstep. I think its throat was slit."

Matt stood up behind his desk, his body tensed, looking as if he wanted to leap over it. "Are you okay? Kat?" he asked, looking over at the dog, his voice trembling with what seemed to Gaby to be suppressed anger.

"Kat was barking and scratching at the door when I came home," Gaby answered, leaning down to rub the dog's head where she lay at Gaby's feet. "I opened the back door to let her out of the house and brought her with me. She seems nervous, but is fine other-wise. I am, frankly, a wreck. Like the other note, the one I showed you, this came out of the blue." She ran her fingers through her hair, then took a deep breath to calm herself and quiet her voice, which threatened to rise to the border of hysteria. Once she had composed herself a bit, she continued. "I knew enough not to touch anything. I didn't go into the house, so I don't know if anything was disturbed—that is, whether anyone came in, though I some-how doubt it."

Matt grabbed the belt holding assorted police paraphernalia he usually wore on duty and buckled it on. Kat immediately stood in response to the trooper's actions. "I need to head out there to take a look," he said briskly, his tone now more official. "Follow me, but stay in your car with Kat until I come to get you. I'll need you to look over the cottage interior with me to see if there's any sign of someone getting in."

Gaby nodded, followed Matt out of his office, then headed to her car while he locked up. She waited until he had pulled the cruiser out of its parking spot, then drove behind him as he made his way to Pine Hill Road, which eventually led to Beaver Trail and Gaby's home.

As she drove, her thoughts were in a jumble. Who had left the note? Why the dead animal? What kind of crazy person kills a cat to make a point, if that's what was intended? Was Matt upset with her or just with what she had reported? Or was he upset she had ignored his previous warning that she might be in danger? Gaby knew such thinking was futile, but the questions kept tumbling around as she drove and continued as she sat in her Subaru with Kat, parked next to the cruiser.

She watched as Matt headed toward the cottage, snapping pictures of the front door with its note and of the dead animal lying on her doorstep, then circling the cottage while snapping pictures of the areas around her house. Returning to the cruiser, he got in it and lifted his radio, presumably calling the barracks covering this section of Connecticut to describe the incident and alert them to the photographs he was sending over the small onboard computer that had become standard equipment for the police.

Watching his initial methodical processing of the scene melted her heart. Though she was certain he approached each of the cases he encountered with the same degree of professionalism and concern his actions were demonstrating here, she felt protected by his mere presence. At the same time, the whole situation increased the level of nervousness she already was feeling, especially since she was left unable to take any action other than to rub Kat's head and hug her in an effort to calm her nerves as well as the dog's.

It was well over half an hour before Matt came over to her car and asked her to come into the house with him using the back door. He was silent as they went through the cottage's few rooms together, Kat trailing behind them, then returning to the kitchen where they had started. Nothing had been disturbed. There was, thankfully, no evidence that anyone had actually entered the property.

"You were out there a long time. Did you find anything?"

"The dead cat looks pretty emaciated—possibly a stray. And whoever killed it did the deed before they brought that poor animal here. There's no blood that I could see. There are some signs that the cat died before its neck was slashed, possibly hit by a car. We'll have to wait for the specialists at the barracks to get here to process the scene," Matt replied. "They'll want to see the original note you got from Helen back at the café as well as contact information for anyone who has handled it, so perhaps you could tend to that. In the meantime, I'll wait in the cruiser for the state investigators to arrive."

"Can't you stay here? Have a cup of coffee at least?" Gaby asked, keeping her voice low and her eyes away from Matt in an effort to control her nerves, afraid he might reject her request.

"Sure," he replied, pulling a chair away from the kitchen table and sitting down.

She went through the steps of brewing a fresh pot of coffee and, while it perked, went into her office to retrieve the note and Carl Grant's contact information. Laying these on the table when she returned, she asked, "Why do you have to call every incident like this into the barracks? Didn't they teach you how to process a scene in trooper school?" She knew her remark was a bit flippant but didn't want to reveal how much she appreciated him staying in the house.

Matt laughed. "Yes, the academy provides the bare bones of the processes necessary for a thorough investigation, similar to what I learned as an MP in the Marines and a cop in the NYPD. But the reality is that no one trooper could develop the level or scope of expertise required to process a scene thoroughly—even a relatively simple one like this.

"Actually," he continued, "it's both the drawback and the benefit of Connecticut's resident state trooper program. A town the size of Woodson Falls wouldn't be able to afford a full-scale police department like they have in, say, Prescott. Instead, a town served by a resident state trooper relies on the expertise available at the state level, which often is far more sophisticated than what's available at the town level. The trade-off is the time it takes for the state investigators to travel to the scene.

"My role is more in the order of keeping the peace—handling the small stuff, deescalating problems, and identifying potential crimes that require the involvement of the state police."

Gaby poured the brewed coffee into two mugs and sat across from the trooper. Taking a deep breath, she said, "I'm sorry I was so obstinate before about the whole thing with the first note. And I'm really sorry I left the café so abruptly the other night. It's hard for me to explain."

Matt sipped his coffee, his intense blue eyes gazing at her over the rim of the mug, but saying nothing.

"Like I told you back then, I didn't want whatever the note represented to interfere with our friendship." Matt remained silent, looking as though he was trying hard not to smile at her words. "Also, I was certain that the note was referring to something Joe had done, and I guess I didn't want you to be the one who uncovered anything that would tarnish the semi-idolized image I had of him, especially after he was killed. I know it probably doesn't make much sense to you and, to be honest, it doesn't to me right now. But there it is." She took a sip of her coffee and looked up at Matt. "So, I apologize for being so pigheaded."

The silence between them grew over the next several minutes. Then Matt put down his coffee mug and said, "Okay. I get it, but as long as we're here in your home, where you can't run off, I want to tell you something."

"Okay."

"Despite your insistence that the note referred to something your husband was involved with, I continued to believe there was a good chance the note and the attack that killed Joe were aimed directly at you."

Gaby sighed and shook her head, but said nothing.

"I've been doing some poking around, Gaby. Does the name Gunther Grossmann ring any bells?"

Chapter 19

"Gʀᴏssᴍᴀɴɴ? Don't think I've heard of him," Gaby said, pouring them each another mugful of coffee. "Is he from around here?"

"No, or at least I don't think so," Matt replied. After a long pause, he sat back and added, "I've been poking around a bit in your past life, particularly your years teaching at Columbia."

"What! Why would you do that?" Gaby exclaimed.

"Since the original note referred to your husband, I assumed the attack that killed Joe involved something that had happened in New York City around that time. You told me when we first met that you taught philosophy at Columbia prior to becoming an attorney and moving to Woodson Falls."

"You remembered that?"

"Of course I did." Matt smiled at Gaby and took a sip of his coffee. "Actually, I remember a lot about that night," he murmured. Taking another sip of coffee, he continued, "I've been pretty certain all along, seeing as you got that first note so many years after the assault, that its sudden arrival in Woodson Falls probably meant you had been the real target of the attack. That led me to assume something from your time teaching at Columbia might hold some answers."

"So you called someone at Columbia?" She gritted her teeth, trying her best not to show her irritation.

"I thought an in-person visit might yield better results than a phone conversation," he said, ignoring the rising tension evident in her expressive face. "So instead of calling, I went down there."

"Probably wasted your time," Gaby said with a shake of her head. "I doubt anyone there even remembers me."

"Quite the contrary, Gaby. At least the person I spoke with, the Philosophy Department secretary—a Mrs. Devereau—has fond memories of you."

"Marge Devereau? She's still there? How sweet of her to remember me! She was a love. Always willing to help me out in a pinch."

"I guess the feeling was mutual. She said you were always helpful to students. Even agreed to see the desperate ones outside your office hours, which I take was unusual."

"Hmm… Guess so, but back then, I figured those students were paying a fortune on tuition and should at least get a little bang for the bucks they were investing."

Matt laughed. "She was sorry you didn't return to the university after Joe died. In any event, she told me that this Gunther Grossmann person was trying to connect with you. He's been calling or dropping in every now and then, up until a few months ago. She told me he had said something about wanting to let you know what an impact you had on his career."

"Oh? I just can't recall the name off the top of my head. Did she describe him?"

"About my height, but slimmer. Hair a bit darker than mine. Reddish beard. Horn-rimmed glasses. Nothing special that stood out for her."

"Tall, dark hair, beard… I'll have to think. But would he have looked the same six years ago?"

"Possibly… Possibly not… Anyway," Matt continued, "apparently it's the office policy not to give out personal information about faculty members, though she thinks she did mention that you had gone to law school and eventually moved somewhere up north. Nothing specific."

"Yeah. Lots of crazies in the city, as you know better than I. We all felt it was wise to keep personal information private, protected like students' data. Actually, I'm surprised Marge said as much as she did."

"She told me she made a note of Gunther's name and phone number and said she'd pass along the information if you ever called her. Which apparently you didn't."

"No, I haven't reconnected with the department in quite a while, though I had to keep my address current with Personnel to ensure I'd be able to collect my retirement benefits down the line. But I doubt anything Marge said was of any help to this Gunther person. And I certainly don't see any connection with Joe's death."

"I did ask when Grossmann had been a student in the department. She looked into the records she had on her computer, but couldn't find the name. Said she didn't think he was a philosophy major, but may have taken a course or two, which was harder to determine. She gave me his phone number to pass along to you."

"I'll comb my memory, but right now, the name means nothing to me. And without any recollection of this person, I wouldn't call him."

Matt got up and put his mug in the sink. "Better get outside to greet the state folks when they arrive. No excuse for being in here, like with the mess at 9 Donovan's Way. I got a bit of grief over staying in the house with you then instead of monitoring the scene of the crime."

After he left, Gaby finished her coffee and washed their used mugs, setting them in the drainer to dry. She wondered why she continued to be so irritated at Matt's insistence that she might well be the target of the stranger's attack. When she needed his help with this incident, she had apologized to him, but now it seemed it may or may not be related to the first note or the attack on Joe. She was starting to wonder if he might be right. She hoped she had adequately concealed her touchiness about the issue.

Going to the front window of the cottage, Gaby watched as the state investigators arrived and went through the same steps Matt had, this time removing the note from her door with gloved hands and placing it in a plastic bag after taking additional pictures of it. The dead animal also was photographed from several angles before being scooped up with as little disturbance as possible and placed in what looked like a scaled-down body bag.

After the state investigators had processed the scene and two of them had returned to their vehicle, Gaby heard a rap on the front door. Opening it, she invited Matt and a man she recognized as Detective Brendan Fisher from Major Crimes into the house. They'd met at 9 Donovan's Way in connection with that case.

"Well, well, Ms. Quinn. We meet again," Fisher greeted her. "In a somewhat different position this time, no?"

"Indeed," Gaby said, leading them into the living room, Kat trailing behind as usual. "Please have a seat. Officer Thomas told me you would want the note I received a few weeks ago to compare with this one. It's in the kitchen. I'll bring it right in."

"Thanks," he said, taking a seat in a chair next to the sofa.

She retrieved the note and handed it to Fisher, who placed it in a plastic evidence bag, writing something on the label affixed to it. "I showed it to a friend of mine in New York. His name is Carl Grant. Here's his contact information too in the event you need to take his fingerprints for comparison purposes. Officer Thomas and I are the only other people who handled the note. It was still in an envelope when the waitress at the Sunshine Café gave it to me. Her name is Helen Wilson."

"Thank you. Very helpful," Fisher said, settling back in the chair and pulling out a notebook. "Now, I know you already answered these questions for Officer Thomas, but can you tell me exactly how you found the note on your door and the dead animal below it, and what you did once you saw them?"

Gaby went through the information as she had with Matt, being careful to explain the pains she had taken so as not to disturb the scene. Fisher nodded as she spoke, jotting down notes without interrupting her account with questions. When it was clear that Gaby had concluded her report, he asked, "And what do you make of the cat?"

Kat was lying at Matt's feet. She perked her ears and barked upon hearing her name.

"Oh, no!" Gaby said, her stomach sinking. Looking over at Matt, she asked, "Do you think…?"

Matt shrugged his shoulders in response, petting the dog and turning to Fisher to explain. "Katrina here is Ms. Quinn's emotional support dog. She calls her Kat. It may just be an odd coincidence, but the note may be threatening more than Ms. Quinn."

Making no comment about the dynamic between Gaby and Matt, if he was even aware of it, Fisher said, "In any case, given the threat implied in these two notes, you may want to request an increase in patrols of this area, Thomas." Turning to Gaby, Fisher added, "I'm not sure what will come of our analysis of this evidence, but I'll keep you and the trooper here informed of anything we find. In the meantime, you'll want to keep your dog close and your doors and windows locked, even in this hot weather."

"That's exactly what I intend to do," Gaby answered, showing both Matt and Fisher out.

The day had clouded over as evening fell. Her mood mirrored the gloomy sky as she prepared dinner for Kat and herself.

Chapter 20

OVER THE WEEK following her lunch with Nell, Gaby heard nothing from the fire marshal or the medical examiner concerning the explosion at Winston Pinkham's home or about his death. Brendan Fisher, with the state's Major Crimes Unit, called several days after the investigators were at her house. Experts had determined that the two notes Gaby received were most likely written by the same person and both bore the same fingerprints. However, whoever penned the notes never had been fingerprinted and so couldn't be identified. A necropsy of the dead cat indicated it had been killed when it was hit by a car and had already died before its neck was slashed.

This news, as well as the lack of anything substantive on Pinkham, left Gaby anxious. Someone was out there, possibly looking to harm Kat, and perhaps her too. She vowed to increase her vigilance, although she already was securing the cottage and taking the dog with her whenever she left home. She even went out with Kat on her visits to the woods, keeping watch in case anyone approached the dog. She had considered asking a friend to keep Kat for the next several days until she knew something about the person who had left the note and dead cat at her door, but couldn't imagine how lost she would feel without her furry companion at her side, especially now.

Then there was the pending issue of Pinkham's estate, which she was eager to open. Her job as executor would be complicated and time-consuming, but all she could do at this point was finish the other cases she had taken on so she would be able to focus on the work necessary to administer Pinkham's estate.

Matt called a week after the incident at her cottage. The fire marshal, Brian Mayfield, and he had information on the explosion and Pinkham's death and wanted to set up a meeting with her.

"The sooner the better," Gaby responded, happy to hear that there was some movement on that front. "When are you both available?"

"How about tomorrow? We can be at your house at ten if that would work for you."

"I'll make it work. Move a few things around. No problem. As sad as I am about Win's death, I'm relieved that I'll be able to start the estate work."

Matt hesitated before saying, "Gaby, I'm sorry. I wanted to tell you in person, but… it looks like Pinkham was murdered. We'll go over the details leading to that conclusion tomorrow, but I'm sure it adds a wrinkle to an already complicated situation."

"Oh, no! Who would want to kill dear old Mr. Pinkham?"

"I'm really sorry, Gab. You just sounded so happy to be able to move ahead with the estate. I didn't want you to be caught off guard tomorrow. I would have come over as soon as I got the news this morning, but Mayfield thinks it best to talk with you together."

"How awful! Who would do such a thing?" she repeated.

"That's the big question. We can brainstorm possibilities at some point, maybe after Mayfield leaves tomorrow. That is, if you have the time."

"Of course. It's just… with the note, the dead cat, then this…"

"I wish I could come over now, but I've got a pile of reports due tomorrow that I've got to work on."

"That's okay. I may be better off alone with my misery. Thanks for the heads up. Guess I'll see you tomorrow," Gaby said, hanging up.

The fire marshal and trooper arrived in separate vehicles promptly at ten the following morning. Gaby led the men into the den after offering them coffee, which they declined. Matt was holding a brown manila envelope that she hoped contained the certified death certificates for Pinkham.

Brian Mayfield spoke first. "As I mentioned when we met previously, we found some irregularities at the 2 Sunrise Trail scene during the investigation following the explosion. These irregularities led us to the conclusion that the explosion had been deliberate, but there was no indication of a motive for setting it off. Some gas explosions occur due to deliberate neglect by building owners who are eager to dislodge tenants for one reason or another. When neglect proves insufficient to lead to an explosion, the owners find a way to make it happen. Other events like this are set in motion to collect the insurance money on a structure where the owner is in financial distress. Neither of these motives seemed to apply here."

"What did you find?" Gaby asked impatiently.

"In addition to the oxygen concentrator setting being unusually high, which I believe I mentioned at our last meeting, we found that the pipeline from the propane tank into the house had been cut."

"Leading to a gas leak within the house," Gaby said, completing the fire marshal's statement for him. "Then Mr. Pinkham lit a cigarette and… boom?"

Matt spoke up. "We don't think so." He tapped the manila envelope he was holding against his knee. "The medical examiner uncovered several things. First, there was no evidence of smoke in Pinkham's lungs despite his body being badly burned. That suggests he died before the explosion occurred. Second, his jugular artery—the blood vessel in the neck leading to the brain—had been severed."

"His body was burned, and badly. How would the medical examiner discover that?" Gaby asked.

"Many times, they wouldn't. But in addition to the severed blood vessel, there was an unusual indentation on a vertebra—one of the neck bones. Whatever was used to cut the jugular artery—most likely a large knife—was swung with sufficient force to nick the bone when the artery was severed. Any blood evidence of that was destroyed in the fire. The indentation on the bone most certainly wasn't caused by something during the explosion. There was no evidence of pre-death blunt force trauma that could be responsible for the damage that was found."

"How gruesome!" Gaby felt her panic rise as she took in the information that Pinkham's death had involved a large knife—as did Joe's so long ago. When combined with the fact that the dead animal left at her doorstep also had its neck cut, she didn't know how much more she could take.

Mayfield picked up the discussion again. "The investigation is ongoing and involves both the Major Crimes Unit and the Fire and Explosion Investigative Unit, but we're likely to need to include you to some degree, considering how close you were to Pinkham. Officer Thomas has a copy of the summary report from the medical examiner along with copies of the death certificate, which I understand you were waiting for to initiate probate. I'm sorry about all this," Mayfield added, hands on his knees, ready to stand and leave.

"Just a minute!" Gaby exclaimed. "I'm confused. If Win's—Pinkham's—smoking didn't set off the explosion, if he was dead before it happened, why wasn't the person who murdered Pinkham killed in the explosion?"

"Easy," answered Mayfield. "We've seen it before. There was a case not long ago in Prescott, matter of fact. The perpetrator allows enough time for gas to fill the building, then places a phone call to the victim. The spark generated by that call is all that's needed to set off the explosion. That is, if the phone is a landline, which I'm assuming is the case here. Wouldn't work with a cell phone unless the perp had set a detonator, and we found no evidence of that."

"Win did use a landline with a portable handset. He didn't want a cell phone and with reception being pretty spotty in Woodson Falls, I never pressed the issue."

"Good to have that confirmed. We'll check his phone records to see if we can trace the call. In any event, the arsonist—in this case, most likely also the murderer—can be far away before the building explodes. In the situation at Sunrise Trail, by setting the oxygen condenser at its highest level, the perp accelerated the flow of oxygen into the house, which supported the fire and explosion that occurred."

Mayfield stood. Matt and Gaby rose with him. As they made their way back to the front door, Matt said, "I'm going to talk with Ms. Quinn a bit more, Brian. Try to get an idea of people who might have wanted Pinkham dead. See you back at the station."

"No problem. You have a good day, Ms. Quinn, and thank you for arranging to see us."

As Mayfield made his way down the flagstone walk, Gaby turned to Matt. "I appreciate your staying behind, but I'm not sure I can be of any help in this."

"Let's go back to the den. I'll ask you some questions and see where that takes us."

Kat trailed behind them as they made their way to Gaby's favorite room, the same room she and Matt had been in when she told him how her face had been scarred. She colored a bit at the memory of Matt hugging her when she finally felt ready to talk about Joe.

"Gaby, please know I'm aware of how upsetting this is to you. Not only to lose a longtime client you were fond of, but also the similarities to your husband's death in the way Pinkham was killed."

"To say nothing of the dead cat at my door. I'm working hard to control my panic, but I'm finding it hard to even think."

"I can appreciate that, but the sooner we can begin an investigation into who might have done this, the more likely we'll be able to identify the killer."

"I'll try. Win knew a lot of people, but those living near enough to Woodson Falls to have done this are few and far between."

"Okay. Where do you want to start?"

Chapter 21

"You sure you don't want a cup of coffee?" Gaby asked Matt before they settled in to talk.

"No, I'm fine. But you go ahead."

"I'll just get a bottle of water. Be right back," Gaby said, heading into the kitchen.

When she returned, she nestled into the sofa and took a long sip of water before beginning. Even on a hot July day, the warmth of the colors she had chosen for this room helped to calm her nerves. She felt ready to provide whatever information she could in the hope she might contribute to solving the mystery surrounding Pinkham's murder.

"Here goes," she began. "Win was involved with the local land trust. Had been for many years. He was serving as their development coordinator, handling large donations for the purchase of conservation easements and parcels of land as well as maintenance of land trust properties. The land trust's executive director, Val— Percival, actually—Conway, has been a pain in my side recently, so he comes to mind first. He didn't have much nice to say about Win, although he did use his nickname, suggesting a close, even affectionate relationship, but I sensed more annoyance with the issues he attributed to Win hanging on to his role with the land trust rather than actual hostility toward him.

"Win also had dealings with the prior land trust treasurer, Alfred Prunagle, but apparently he's moved to Texas, which led to the problems Win was having with his financial records. I think I told you about that a while back, when we met for supper."

Matt looked up at Gaby for a moment, then back down to his notebook. "I take it this Conway person lives in Woodson Falls?"

"Yes."

"You say he's been a pain. In what way? Other than expressing his annoyance at Pinkham."

"Win told me Conway had been pressuring him to deed over the property adjoining his house on Sunrise Trail to the land trust. That had been Pinkham's original intent but, like many people who lived during the Depression, he was concerned about having enough money to see him through his final years. He had decided to subdivide the property to create six lots he could sell, assuming by doing that he could monetize the value of the raw land. He hadn't counted on the significant costs of creating the subdivision and, when he realized how much he was spending on the work, he decided he had to complete the project to at least recoup his investment.

"Conway called me the day after the explosion. He assumed Win had died in the blast and asked if his will provided a legacy for the land trust."

"Does it?" Matt asked.

"Not in his will, but Win did provide for the land trust through a sizable charitable remainder trust that paid him an annuity during his lifetime. Whatever was left, which I recently learned is a significant amount of money, will go to the land trust. While I assumed, as Conway did, that it was Win's body in the rubble at Sunrise Trail following the explosion, that hadn't been verified yet by the medical examiner, so I didn't tell Conway about the trust. I thought it was a bit ghoulish for him to be asking about what Win might have provided for the land trust in his will when his death hadn't been confirmed yet.

"Conway seems totally focused on raising funds and acquiring land for the trust. He's embarked on a major campaign to purchase and preserve a large tract of land in the north end of town. Win was under the impression Conway eventually wanted to merge the Woodson Falls Land Trust with other smaller trusts in the area so he could rule a bigger roost. It's possible Conway viewed Win's opposition to his plan as thwarting his hope of eventually securing a paid position with a large conglomerate. His current role is only part-time, and since the Woodson Falls Land Trust is relatively small, I'm sure he isn't being paid much."

"Okay. It's worth checking out this Conway character's whereabouts once we're able to zero in on when Pinkham was killed. We'll need that timeline as a basis for evaluating the alibis of any potential suspects. Who else?"

"There's Win's accountant and his bookkeeper, who visited at regular intervals, and Carolyn Gleason, who did his shopping and cleaning. None of them had any reason to want Win dead that I know of. Same goes for the people who volunteer for Friendly Drivers, the local non-profit that transports folks like Win to medical appointments. They were involved in taking him to various doctors. I filled in on occasion when they didn't have an available driver."

"All-around do-gooder, aren't you?" Matt commented with a gentle smile. "Who else?"

"Well, there are the people who were involved in the subdivision he was working on, primarily Blackberry Hill Engineering, although I think their work is done. Oh, and there are two so-called 'friends,' Bud Wiseman and Adam Samuelson. I have their address—in Prescott—since they're mentioned in Win's will. I'll get them for you as soon as we're finished.

"I'm not sure why Win was involved with such obviously disreputable people, but he had offered them each a substantial discount on a selected lot in the subdivision in exchange for their help with the project. He mentioned to me that the two men had been bugging him about leaving the lots to them outright through his will if he passed away before they purchased them or giving them a steeper discount on the cost of the lots than the twenty percent he had offered in return for their help with the subdivision process—which was no help at all in my estimation. In any event, the twenty-percent discount carries through in Win's will. But I'm not even sure they have the funds to go through with the purchase."

"Do you think either of them might have been involved with this?"

"Based on what Mayfield was saying, whoever killed Win and orchestrated the explosion had to know enough to be dangerous. I just don't think either Adam or Bud is sophisticated enough to pull off such a complicated scheme, but who knows?"

"Still worth checking out. That's a good start, Gab. Anyone else you can think of?"

"Win told me he had some friends from New York visiting recently. They arrived on the Thursday before the Fourth, but were supposed to have left midday on Sunday, the day of the town's parade. I have no idea who they were."

"Well, that'll be interesting to investigate!"

"I don't even know where you would begin."

Matt laughed. "For someone you seemed to describe as something of a recluse, it appears he had a lot of folks in his social circle. Would you happen to have a picture of Pinkham?"

"No, and I wouldn't even know how to describe him except as a kind old man. The land trust may have a photo or two of Win as a member of the board of directors and longtime volunteer. And I believe he drove at one time, so there may be a driver's license picture available from the DMV."

"Good thoughts," Matt said, putting away the notebook in which he was jotting down the information she was giving him.

Gaby smiled, reminded of how well she and Matt had worked together on the case at 9 Donovan's Way. This felt almost the same, except for her closeness to the victim.

"Let me get the information on Adam and Bud," Gaby said, getting up and heading to her office. When she returned, she said, "You probably know that Detective Fisher came by late last week to update me on the investigation into the note on my door. I'm sure he talked with you about that."

Matt nodded.

"Have you heard anything more? I'm kind of on pins and needles. I think knowing something concrete would help to calm my nerves a bit."

"Afraid there's nothing new on that front. Like the situation with the explosion and your client's death, there's little substantive to go on." Matt paused. "Have you given any thought to the name I mentioned—Gunther Grossmann?"

Gaby stiffened, then shook her head. "With all this stuff with Win, I really haven't time to shuffle through my memory bank." She gave Matt a weak smile. "I'll get there… one of these days."

Gaby led the trooper to the front door, with Kat padding behind.

"Thanks for taking the time to talk with me," Matt said, turning to face her, "even though you must be upset with the news Brian and I had about your client. You've given me a few leads to pursue in trying to solve this. I really appreciate it."

"No problem," Gaby said, standing in the open door and holding Kat by her collar, knowing the dog was likely to follow Matt to his cruiser.

The trooper started down the walkway, then turned. "Gaby, would you have dinner with me on Saturday evening? I feel we need to clear the air. I know I've upset you, and I don't want to do that."

Gaby's heart skipped a beat as she said, "I'd like that. Let me know when and where."

"Good. How about I pick you up at six?"

"Okay."

Matt continued toward his cruiser, then turned back again. "I'm sure it's not intentional, but… you're messing with my heart, Gaby."

Whoa. Didn't see that coming, she thought with a smile that turned to a grin as she shut the door and leaned against it. *Guess I really* am *out of practice.*

Chapter 22

When Saturday rolled around, Matt picked up Gaby at six as promised. They drove to Westbury, two towns south of Woodson Falls, and parked outside a small, storefront restaurant called Florio's. Matt had reserved a table for two in the window, away from the few other diners in the restaurant.

"I hope you're okay with Italian. They serve incredible northern Italian food here," Matt said.

"Love it," Gaby responded, looking around. "Such a cute place."

The restaurant had—at most—ten tables, each set with a crisp white tablecloth, a small vase with fresh flowers, and a candle in a green glass holder. The lighting was low, reflecting off the deep yellow walls in a pleasant glow. In the background, instrumental music played softly.

A waiter approached with glasses of water, which he placed on their table. "My name's Logan. I'll be your waiter this evening. Can I get you folks anything to drink?"

"Gaby?" Matt asked.

"A sauvignon blanc, please," she said to the waiter.

"Same," Matt said.

"Our specials today are a zuppa Tuscana, a Tuscan version of minestrone, and bruschetta made with fresh tomatoes, garlic and basil to start," Logan announced. "For the main course, we're offering a grilled veal chop served with asparagus and new potatoes. Our fresh fish of the day is a grilled snapper served with asparagus and orecchiette. I'll be right back with your wines."

Matt smiled at Gaby. "So, did you finally get started on Pinkham's estate?"

"Yes, but I was horrified to learn he had been murdered. I've never had to check the box on the probate application indicating a wrongful death, although that's pretty much irrelevant in this case."

"What do you mean?"

"A wrongful death usually involves an accidental death, like a plane crash, where there's the possibility of a financial award to the estate of the person who died. With Win having been murdered, while obviously wrongful, there won't be an insurance settlement and that's what the probate court really is concerned with."

"I see."

Logan returned with their wine, setting the glasses on the table. "I'll be right back with some bread."

After the waiter had delivered the promised basket of assorted warm rolls and sliced focaccia along with a generous square of butter sitting in a bath of olive oil and garnished with a sprig of thyme, Gaby continued, "I was able to get started with a bit of prep work even before you brought the certified death certificates. They just allowed me to begin the estate administration process formally. The court requires the executor to send certain documents as well as a copy of the will to every heir and beneficiary, so I had all of that set up and ready to go. Everything copied and the envelopes addressed, along with a cover letter explaining the process."

"You sound relieved."

"With everything that's been going on, it was good to have busy work to focus on. Otherwise, I'd be obsessing about Win's death."

"To say nothing of the note on your door."

"That, too."

Their waiter brought their wine, then asked if they had any questions about the menu or if they were ready to order.

"Gaby?"

"I'll skip the appetizer and start with the house salad instead. And I'd like the snapper for the main course."

"Sir?"

"I'll start with the soup special and then the veal chop. Thank you," Matt answered, handing their menus back to the waiter.

Matt lifted his glass. "To solving cases."

Gaby smiled and clinked her glass against his. "To solving cases." Tempted though she was to add "and clearing the air," she decided to wait until Matt broached the subject leading to his dinner invitation.

Taking a sip of his wine, Matt began. "I know I've offended you. Probably by being overprotective. I've tried to hold back, but I've always had an urge to protect the people I care about. Actually, even people I don't care about. It's probably why I ended up in law enforcement. So, force of habit to want to protect you when I sense you're in danger."

"I get that, but…"

Matt put his hand up to stop her. "If you'll just bear with me for a minute, I need to explain this to you."

"Okay."

"My younger brother was born with Down's syndrome. As Billy's big brother, I felt I should be the one to protect him from potential attacks by other kids. My size alone was a deterrent, but I got into the habit of glaring at kids or standing between them and my brother if I had any thought they might be approaching Billy to mess with him."

"Oh, my! I can understand how that would affect you, but…"

Logan returned with their starters.

Matt chuckled as the waiter left again. "Restaurants do offer neutral territory, but it's hard to keep a conversation going."

"So true," Gaby answered, thinking back to her lunch with Nell earlier in the week. "I really appreciate your concern for my safety, Matt. I guess it's just that I worked so hard to regain some sense of autonomy and self-control despite the lingering effects of the PTSD I told you about.

"It's hard for me to depend on someone else again after the pain of losing Joe, to appear vulnerable and needy. I had to pick up the pieces of my shattered life after Joe died, and frankly, the possibility of going through that again scares me." She refrained from telling Matt that his work as a trooper was a major factor for her fear and likely contributed to her pushing him away when she'd rather hold him close.

She paused. "As far as the note warning me not to probe into Joe's death goes, I guess I feel I need to prove that I can take care of myself. Plus, I have to admit, I'd hate it if you ended up uncovering something unsavory about Joe."

Matt nodded his understanding.

She smiled. "Don't let your soup get cold," she added as Logan approached with a giant pepper grinder.

"Fresh pepper, ma'am?"

"Just a touch, thanks."

They ate for a while, Matt finishing his soup before she was done with her salad. Taking another sip of his wine, he said, "Vulnerable. That's the impression I got when I first met you at the Prescott police station. But then I saw how you dealt with that young man. You were so straightforward in pleading his case, so gentle in dealing with him. You seemed vulnerable—kind of like a fish out of water—and yet somehow resilient."

Gaby chuckled. "I *felt* like a fish out of water. I had never dealt with a criminal case before. But I knew I had to help poor Walter. His mother was so worried."

"Then when I found you later, standing in the freezing rain with your car pushed off the road, I thought again that you were vulnerable. You certainly were shivering. But instead of breaking down in tears, you were angry. You seemed determined to find out who would do such a thing—just drive off after hitting another vehicle. Each time I found myself thinking you were vulnerable, you proved me wrong with how strong you are."

Logan returned, took away their appetizer plates, returning a short while later with their entrées. "Another wine for either of you?" he asked, sliding a steak knife into Matt's place setting.

Gaby looked at Matt and said, "Yes, I'd like that. Another sauvignon blanc, please."

"I'll switch to a cabernet, please." After Logan left, he said, "Let's eat. Pick this up later."

A few minutes passed, then Gaby remarked, "This is delicious! Such subtle flavors and cooked perfectly. Fish can be hard to get right. This is excellent!"

"I'm glad. A friend brought me here a while back, and I thought you might enjoy it."

They continued to eat, making small talk. Gaby felt more at ease as the evening progressed, less concerned it would turn into one more confrontation about her safety now that she had a better sense of where Matt was coming from and had a chance to articulate her need to control situations she found herself in.

After they were finished eating, had declined dessert, and ordered coffee, Matt picked up the conversation.

"This is hard for me, so please, let me just get it out." Matt took a sip of his wine and sat back. "I told you back when we were working on the Lakeview Terrace thing that my daughter Julia was killed in a hit-and-run accident that badly injured my wife, who was pregnant with our son, and that she died a few days after Julia. Brenda was the only woman I ever dated. We were high school sweethearts and even went to the same college, where we continued our relationship.

"In my sophomore year, I realized I wasn't sure what I wanted to do when I graduated—had no clue what to major in. Continuing in school felt like I was wasting my parents' money and my time. I had signed up for ROTC, so it seemed logical to drop out and join the Marines. I kept in touch with Brenda, and after I served my four-year enlistment, I returned home, joined the NYPD, and married her.

"Something died in me when I lost Brenda and Julia. People kept saying it was 'time to move on,' but even more than being totally insensitive to the depth of loss I was experiencing, it felt like 'moving on' would be disloyal to Brenda and Julia. I felt like having a relationship with someone else would mean abandoning my one-and-only family."

Gaby started to respond, but once again, Matt put up his hand to stop her.

"Back in the spring, when I was on that fishing trip in Florida, I talked to my friend Don a bit about you, about how comfortable I felt working with you. And Don just said I deserved a life. Somehow, framing it that way felt different from 'moving on.' It got me thinking that maybe I was dishonoring what Brenda and I had together by *not* living fully."

He paused, finishing his wine before continuing. "I really like you, Gaby. Yet you seem to be pushing me away. And if that's what you want… just the occasional professional relationship of the 'law and order' sort, then I'll just have to accept that."

"Matt," Gaby started to say, but he interrupted her.

"Can I say something without you getting all ruffled and defensive? I want to protect you. I want… God … I don't know just what I want, but I want more than that."

Matt looked at her with a longing that nearly broke her heart.

"I do, too," she whispered.

Chapter 23

THE PHONE CALLS began the following week.

"Law offices. Gabriella Quinn speaking," she announced to Tuesday's caller.

"It's Adam Samuelson, Attorney Quinn. Remember me from that meeting about Pinky's subdivision?"

"Yes?"

"Well, I just received the stuff you mailed out with Pinky's will."

"As a beneficiary of Mr. Pinkham's estate, under the terms of the will, you're entitled to receive a copy of that document, along with other forms submitted to the probate court."

"I think you made a mistake and sent out an old version of Pinky's will. He promised me and Bud that, because of all the help we gave him over the years in working for the land trust— for nothing—if he died before we bought the lots we picked out in the Sunrise Hills subdivision, he was planning on leaving us the lots outright rather than at a discount. That's not in the copy of the will you sent us."

"I think it's you who are mistaken, Mr. Samuelson. The copy of the will I sent to you and Mr. Pinkham's other beneficiaries is the last one he made. He told me you and Mr. Wiseman had asked

126

him to leave those lots to you through his will, but he certainly hadn't acted on your request before he died."

"You're wrong! Or else you twisted Pinky's arm to stop him from giving us those lots for free."

"I did no such thing!" Gaby exclaimed. Collecting herself, she continued, "However, if you have a question about the validity of the will, you'll have the opportunity to make your case before the probate court. You'll be receiving a hearing notice allowing you to state your claim, but you better be able to prove it to the court's satisfaction. Just your saying so won't cut it."

"You can be sure me and Bud will be there. We have a letter from Pinky himself promising us those lots."

"Good luck with that," Gaby said, hanging up and shaking her head. She had thought she was done with Adam and Bud once the town had approved the subdivision Pinkham was creating on land he'd owned since he first arrived in Woodson Falls many years ago.

While Pinkham's will reflected his desire that Adam and Bud each receive a discount on a specified lot in the subdivision, a real estate agent would handle those transactions, with Gaby involved only at the closings. It would be interesting to see whether either man was able to pay even the discounted price of the lots once they were appraised and placed on the market. Not for the first time, she wondered why Win would surround himself with such oddballs as Adam Samuelson and Bud Wiseman and whether other similar characters would emerge now that Win had died.

She had returned to her work when the phone rang again. This time, it was Percival Conway calling.

"Good afternoon, Ms. Quinn. Val Conway here, with the Woodson Falls Land Trust?"

"How can I help you, Mr. Conway?"

"I received your mailing with old Pinkham's will. Perhaps you can explain just what is meant by the term 'contingent' as it is used here to refer to the land trust? I had assumed Win left a substantial gift to the WFLT."

"Actually, he did. Another attorney—a Daniel Jackson with Swift, Cooke & Jackson in Westbury—drafted a charitable remainder trust on Mr. Pinkham's behalf. The trust paid Mr. Pinkham an annuity during his lifetime, with the balance to be paid to the Woodson Falls Land Trust upon Pinkham's death. When I last checked, right after the explosion at 2 Sunrise Trail, the balance in the account was well over five hundred thousand dollars. Those funds will be paid over to the land trust after the probate court has determined that all expenses required by law to be paid out of a decedent's estate, as well as any claims against estate assets, have been satisfied.

"But to answer your question, the section of Mr. Pinkham's will referencing the land trust as a contingent beneficiary usually is referred to as the 'common disaster' clause, to ensure estate assets go somewhere if all the decedent's heirs and beneficiaries die before Pinkham. Given the sheer numbers and locations of Mr. Pinkham's named heirs and beneficiaries, it was highly unlikely that the common disaster clause would come into effect, and it won't now."

"Well then," Conway sniffed, "at least the land trust will be getting something." He paused, then asked, "And what of the Sunrise Hills subdivision? I know the road hasn't been put in as yet, so the land is still pretty much untouched. Have you given any thought to donating that property to the land trust on behalf of the estate, as well as the lot Pinkham's house was on? Save you a lot of time and work marketing the lots."

"Interesting that you should ask. Mr. Pinkham toyed with the idea of creating a codicil to his will, deeding the Sunrise Hills land to the land trust if he passed away before the road was constructed, but he never acted on the thought. As Mr. Pinkham's executor, my duty is to the heirs and beneficiaries named in his will, which means

I am required to make decisions that maximize the value of estate assets for their benefit, regardless of the work that might entail."

"But it's my understanding that donating the Sunrise Hills property to the land trust would result in a substantial deduction against any estate taxes owed to the state and federal governments. Isn't that so?"

"Yes, that's correct. However, while Mr. Pinkham's estate is substantial, its value is still below the allowable exclusion for both state and federal estate taxes, so such a donation would only serve to deprive his heirs and beneficiaries of their rightful share in his estate."

"Oh, well. I certainly did my best to convince old Win to donate the land before he died. I know his original intent was to donate that property to us through his will, but I guess he changed his mind."

"Hmm…" was Gaby's only response, eager to end the conversation.

Two days later, Gaby received another call concerning Pinkham's estate, this time from one of his distant cousins, an Edith Vincent.

"Gabriella Quinn? You're the attorney handling my dear cousin Winston's estate?"

"Yes, Mr. Pinkham named me as executor in his will. You should have received a copy of it by now, along with the filings submitted to the probate court, which must approve the appointment of the estate's executor. That's part of the probate process."

"Well, don't you think a family member would be better suited to handle this matter?"

"What I think really isn't important. It was your cousin's decision."

"Regardless, it seems entirely inappropriate to name a virtual stranger, no offense intended. And I can't believe Winston left a mere five hundred dollars to me and to our cousin Raymond. He must have been in his dotage when he made this will, rest his dear soul. And just a mere four or five months before his death, too."

"Can I help you with something, Ms. Vincent?" Gaby asked, uncertain just what the woman was seeking but suspecting that a will contest was in the offing.

"Raymond and I have discussed the matter after reviewing the documents you sent. We firmly believe Winston was incompetent at the time he made this will and that the probate court should declare it null and void. As the closest family dear Winston had left, we should be named as the proper recipients of his estate, don't you think?"

"Again, Ms. Vincent, what I think is irrelevant. And as Mr. Pinkham's attorney as well as the proposed executor of his estate, it would be inappropriate for me to discuss the matter with you or any other beneficiary beyond the scope of the documents I mailed to you. The probate court will be sending each heir and beneficiary named in the will a hearing notice. The hearing is the proper place to make known your concerns about the validity of Mr. Pinkham's will."

"But I live in Wisconsin! And Raymond is all the way out in Idaho and recovering from a hip replacement!"

"If you and Raymond let the court know you will be unable to attend the hearing in person, I'm certain the judge would accommodate a request to attend by telephone and be happy to accept any evidence you might wish to submit challenging the will or Mr. Pinkham's competency. You might want to retain local counsel to represent your interests to the court, although that's not required."

"Oh dear! That would cost us a pretty penny! Can you recommend anyone? Someone who doesn't charge an arm and a leg?"

"I fear it would be a conflict of interest for me to do so. I suggest you call the Connecticut Bar Association for a list of attorneys in this area who handle probate matters. If you give me a minute, I'll get their number for you."

After Gaby provided the bar association's phone number, which she had to repeat several times for her caller to record accurately, she wished Ms. Vincent a pleasant afternoon and hung up, shaking her head. Though she knew that relatives who had paid little attention to an individual while he was alive often came out of the woodwork to nibble at whatever was left upon his death, the sheer greed such behavior represented still bewildered her.

It was approaching the end of Gaby's workday when Matt called. "Hi, Gaby."

"Hi," she responded, remembering the warmth of his embrace and goodnight kiss when he brought her home from their dinner last Saturday.

"Just wanted you to know we might have a lead on Pinkham's New York visitors."

"That's good news! I've had some interesting phone conversations you probably should know about."

"Want to meet for breakfast tomorrow? Law and order once again," Matt said. Gaby could feel his smile through the phone.

"Café?"

"Of course. Is eight too early for you?"

"Not at all."

"It's a date."

Chapter 24

"I CAN'T BELIEVE you were able to learn something about Win's New York visitors!" Gaby exclaimed, sliding into the booth Matt had taken at the café.

"And good morning to you, too," Matt answered with a smile. "It was Peggy's doing," he said, in response to Gaby's comment. When Matt had asked her whether Pinkham and his visitors were at the café in the days prior to the Sunday of the parade and fireworks, Peggy Huntington, owner of the restaurant, recalled seeing Pinkham with three other men the morning of the parade. "She hadn't seen him in years, but still recognized him."

"Of course I did," Peggy said, coming to their booth with a coffeepot and filling their cups without asking. "Even though so much time has passed and the thick thatch of hair he had way back then was down to a few white strands, that chuckle of his—regardless of his smoker's cough, or maybe because of it—was so distinctive. As soon as I heard his laugh—even though the café was packed with people—I came over to say hello."

"Peggy went over the receipts for that day," Matt explained, "and was able to ferret out their check, which had been paid by one of Pinkham's guests using a credit card. That gave me a name to work with, and I was able to locate his contact information."

"Win was a good man. I can't believe someone killed him. Have you figured out who?"

"Not yet," Gaby answered.

"The case really is in the hands of Major Crimes working with the state's Fire and Explosion Investigative Unit," Matt added. "We're just trying to find information that might be helpful to them."

"How did you meet Mr. Pinkham?" Gaby asked.

"We worked together clearing trails for the land trust, way back when I was still a scout. I did the trail markers as part of my senior project at high school. Win helped a lot with that. He was always ready to lend a hand if it involved the land trust, even though he was only up here on weekends back then." Peggy paused and smiled. "Tried to save people as well as the land. Brought young men from New York up to work on the trails. Not the best and brightest by a long shot, but that was Win. Always fighting for the underdog.

"As a matter of fact, two of those young men—Adam Samuelson and Bud Wiseman—are still in the area. I've seen them in here occasionally. I don't know if they still volunteer for the land trust, but I overheard Win mention to his New York friends that two of the people he recruited for the land trust were helping him with that subdivision he was trying to create. Seems a bit out of character, come to think, that he'd want to develop land even though he was such a conservationist. Guess he had his reasons.

"Are you planning to have a memorial service for him?" she asked Gaby. "He may have been a recluse in his later years, but a lot of folks who've lived in Woodson Falls any length of time certainly would want to have the opportunity to celebrate his life."

"I thought the land trust would want to set that up. I guess I should follow up with them to be sure. Thanks for the reminder."

"No problem. I'll get Helen over here to take your order. Just wanted to say hello to our local crime-busters."

"Thanks, Peggy," Matt said.

"So, were you able to get in touch with one of Win's guests? Or at least the one who paid the check?" Gaby asked Matt once Peggy left to find Helen.

"Not my place," Matt answered. "Passed along the information I gathered to Major Crimes, who will follow up with the NYPD to locate all three men. I'm particularly interested in when they left Sunrise Trail and whether anyone else was with Pinkham around that time. That information would be a big help in pinning down the time of the murder. And having a sense of when Pinkham was killed would enable Major Crimes to check the alibis of any suspects they might identify."

"You don't think any of his visitors were involved in this?" Gaby asked.

"I know it's a possibility, but it's a long shot. In any event, it will be the detectives with Major Crimes who'll have to determine whether they were involved." Matt took a sip of coffee, then asked, "You said you had some calls that might be relevant?"

"Nothing as concrete as you managed to get. More a confirmation of what we talked about after you and Mayfield told me Win had been murdered."

"Anything would be helpful at this point," Matt said.

Helen came by to take their order.

"Two eggs, scrambled, please," Gaby said, "bacon, biscuits, no potatoes."

"And you, officer?"

"Breakfast special, please," Matt answered, "and another splash of coffee when you have time."

"I should just take the chance and bring you both your usual breakfasts. Neither of you ever gets adventurous enough to try something else," Helen said, tucking her order pad in the waistband of her apron.

"I ordered pancakes once, remember?" Gaby said.

"And didn't eat them, if I recall correctly," Helen responded with a smile. "Be right back with more coffee."

"So, who have you heard from?" Matt asked Gaby.

"I didn't think of them when we were talking about potential suspects the other day, but I heard from one of Pinkham's two remaining family members—both cousins. It was an Edith Vincent who called. She was upset that Pinkham left such a small bequest to her and their other cousin."

"How much did he leave them?"

"Five hundred dollars each. I recall Pinkham being peeved that neither of them kept in touch with him beyond an occasional Christmas card. Ms. Vincent claimed Win must have been senile to have left so little to each of them and, beyond that, to have named a 'stranger' as his executor. She wants the probate court to throw out the will, which would mean that Win died intestate and, as his only heirs, she and the other cousin would split the entire estate."

"Could that happen?"

"She and her cousin, a Raymond Pinkham, have every right to contest the will, but it's doubtful they'll be successful. They'd have to prove Win was incompetent, especially since giving them even a small bequest demonstrated that he didn't forget they existed."

"How difficult is it to prove incompetence?"

"I'm pretty sure the court would ask to have Win's primary physician certify that he had dementia or was otherwise incompetent to manage his affairs and that his condition would have prevented him from understanding what he was doing when he signed the will. That's not going to happen. The legal threshold for incompetency is pretty high. If Win had been that disabled, he wouldn't have been able to carry out his day-to-day activities, and that just wasn't true.

"I also include an affidavit with every will I draft in which the witnesses attest that all the legal requirements surrounding the execution of a will have been met."

"Such as?"

"In Connecticut, a will must be signed by two witnesses in the presence of the testator—the person signing the will—and each other. Additionally, the witnesses swear they're witnessing the will at the testator's request, that the testator appears to be of legal age—that's eighteen or older—of 'sound mind and memory and competent,' and that the act of signing the will is voluntary. The affidavit usually suffices to avoid having the probate court seek the testimony of the witnesses, although the judge can always ask for them to provide the same information in person."

"Okay. So this affidavit and a doctor's report take care of the claim of dementia. Why would they care that you were named as executor?"

"Some people assume an executor can play 'fast and loose' with estate assets. That simply isn't the case. It's the job of the executor to fulfill the decedent's wishes as expressed in the will, as well as to pay legally required expenses and any claims made against estate assets. They get paid for the effort, but the court scrutinizes the executor's fee to ensure it isn't excessive."

"So you're the executor, but also the attorney for the estate. Isn't that unusual?" Matt asked.

"It's not uncommon for a person to name their attorney as executor since a lawyer who does estate planning is well versed in the requirements for administering an estate," Gaby answered. "That's particularly true for someone like Win, who had few people close to him. He did ask his accountant to serve in that capacity, but he declined, so Win chose me."

"But doesn't that set up a claim that you're 'double-dipping?'"

"Doing that would certainly get the judge's attention. I usually add just one percent to the usual three-percent fee an executor earns, depending on the complexity of the estate. And Pinkham's is very complex, given the subdivision property that needs to be sold and the work involved to clean up the property on Sunrise Trail and then get it on the market. I'll end up earning every penny of the fee I charge. And I'll maintain time sheets to document the hours I spend on the estate."

"So what is this cousin complaining about?"

"She probably assumes I pushed Win to name me as executor or simply named myself when I drafted the will. Either would be impossible to prove."

"Are you worried about any of this?"

"The will contest? No. It'll just serve to delay the administration of Win's estate. But even with a simple estate, it takes about a year to complete the entire probate process."

"Do you think either of these cousins might have been at all involved in Pinkham's murder?"

"Not unless they hired a hit-man to do the job," Gaby answered with a smile. "Ms. Vincent lives in Wisconsin. The other cousin, who is recovering from hip replacement surgery, lives in Idaho. Both are elderly, as I suspected, given Win's age. So no, I don't think either of them is implicated. Beyond the potential will contest, they are just two among other folks disappointed in the provisions of Win's will."

Chapter 25

AFTER HELEN had brought their breakfasts, Gaby continued sharing her thoughts with Matt. "In any event, I think we can forget the cousins. Do you want to give their contact information to the detective from Major Crimes? Let him rule the pair out?"

"Probably be a good idea," Matt responded, digging into his pancakes after demolishing the egg on top of the stack and pouring a generous serving of syrup on the cakes.

"Okay. I'll give you the addresses for both." She nibbled at a strip of bacon, savoring its crispness and salty taste. "I also heard from Conway—the head of the land trust. Gosh, he's persistent. I can see why Win took such a dislike to the man."

"What was he looking for?"

"Like I mentioned before, I'm required to send Win's will and certain of the probate documents concerning his estate to every heir and beneficiary. The land trust was named as a contingent beneficiary, meaning the trust would receive all the assets in the estate if every heir and beneficiary predeceased Win, which obviously didn't happen. Conway asked what 'contingent' meant, but I'm sure he already knew. Most charitable organizations ask regular donors to consider a gift to the organization as part of their estate planning. He obviously expected Win to provide an outright bequest to the land trust, given his dedication to the organization over the years."

"And he didn't?" Matt asked, sipping his coffee.

"Not through his will," Gaby answered, buttering her biscuit. "But the charitable remainder trust I told you about naming the Woodson Falls Land Trust as the recipient of any remaining assets upon Win's death is worth well over half a million. I don't think Conway knew about it beforehand, and you'd think he'd be pleasantly surprised to get that news."

"But he wasn't?" Matt looked around, signaling Helen for another coffee and the check.

"He started in about the Sunrise Hills subdivision, urging me to donate the property to the land trust rather than develop it, which as Win's executor I'm empowered to do. Donating the property would simplify matters for me, but wouldn't be in the best interests of Win's beneficiaries. My duty is as much to them as it is to follow Win's wishes as expressed in his will.

"Conway had been bugging Win to donate the property to the land trust, even after he'd embarked on the subdivision plan, but Win was convinced he needed the funds generated by the subdivision once the lots were sold to support him until he died. He did toy with the idea of creating a codicil to his will—sort of a P.S.— to donate the Sunrise Hills land to the trust if the road wasn't put in before he died, which would have satisfied Conway and been in keeping with Win's passion for land preservation, but he never acted on that thought.

"I've run into beneficiaries like Edith Vincent, who are looking for more than they received, but I don't understand Conway's obsession with Win's estate. He really has no personal stake in this, at least not that I can see. I can understand being zealous on behalf of a charity, but Conway seems over the top to me."

"Do you like him for Pinkham's murder?" Matt asked, nodding his thanks to Helen for the refill of his coffee and putting some bills on the table to cover the check.

"I'm not sure what his motive would be," Gaby continued. "As I said, he doesn't have an interest in the estate other than as the head of the land trust. He didn't seem to know about the charitable remainder trust, which provides a hefty bequest to an organization the size of the Woodson Falls Land Trust. You'd think he'd be satisfied with that."

"I've already told the detective who's handling the case about Conway as well as those two friends of Win's we talked about. I'm sure they'll ask me for any support they need to better determine if any of them were involved. I've learned along the way that people can have strange motives driving their behavior, however criminal it might be," Matt said, gulping down his coffee then standing. "I need to get over to the office in case anyone's looking for me. How about you come over when you're done with your coffee? You can fill me in on any other calls you might have gotten about Pinkham's estate."

"I'm done. Thanks for breakfast," Gaby said, joining Matt as he headed to the door. "The only others who called were the two friends, Adam and Bud, but I had a thought I wanted to share with you."

They made their way across the green toward the emergency services building. Once they were in Matt's office, Gaby said, "It was Adam who called. He seems to be the spokesman for that pair. Claimed Win had promised he'd give them the lots they wanted in Sunrise Hills outright if he died before the subdivision was completed. Said they had a letter from Win to that effect."

"Do they?"

"I seriously doubt it, but even if they produced a letter, proving it came from Win would be difficult and, legally, it wouldn't change the language in the will. Besides, I'm certain Win would have told me about such a change since it would need to be reflected in his will, which only addressed the discount on the price of the lots he had promised that pair.

"He was careful about keeping his affairs up-to-date." She smiled sadly. "He was a paradox. Told everyone he was at death's door while worrying about whether he'd have enough money to support himself in the coming years."

"Wish I'd met him," Matt said. "Sounds like an interesting character, in a good way. You had something else you wanted to tell me?"

"Just a thought. I said earlier I was pretty sure neither Adam nor Bud was sophisticated enough to pull off Win's murder and the propane explosion that destroyed the house. But what if Win's killer had been trained as a firefighter, even a volunteer firefighter? If they were, they might have been exposed to similar circumstances and known what to do."

"Good thought. I'll add that to my list when I check the backgrounds of the three most likely suspects, which the detective working the case asked me to do while they pursue other leads."

"I'll get out of your hair now," Gaby said, heading to the office door. "I have a pile of work to attend to, and I'm sure you do too. Thanks again for breakfast and for dinner the other night," she added with a smile. "I owe you."

"You can make dinner for me any night of the week."

"You're on!"

Gaby headed home, suddenly concerned about what might await her. Close to three weeks had passed with no sign of whoever left the note and the dead cat at her door, and no further word from the state police investigating the case. She'd grown less cautious over that time, leaving Kat alone in the locked house when she had gone to dinner with Matt last Saturday and then to breakfast this morning. She was relieved when she heard Kat's welcoming bark and saw her perched on the sofa to watch for Gaby's return through the window.

She took some time to cuddle with the dog before letting her out for a trip to the woods, keeping a watchful eye. August was approaching and with it the rising heat and humidity of late summer in Woodson Falls. Kat seemed eager to return to the cooler cottage, following Gaby into the office after lapping at her water bowl.

In the odd moments when she wasn't attending to one of her many law cases or thinking about Pinkham's murder, she had been searching her memories of her days at Columbia University in an effort to dredge up some recollection related to the name Matt had given her: Gunther Grossmann. But nothing popped.

She focused instead on anyone in Woodson Falls or the surrounding towns who might be responsible for the two notes she had received, the most recent tacked to her door above a cat whose throat had been slit, much as Pinkham's had.

Could the cases be related in some way? After all, both the dead animal and her dead client had been killed with a knife, much as Joe had been. Gaby shook her head. It seemed a bit far-fetched to think that one person was responsible for all three incidents.

Way back at the start of the case on Lakeview Terrace, she had spotted a strange man eating at the café and had asked Helen who he might be. The waitress didn't know his name, only that he was working on the old Haverson place in the north end of town. The same man had given Helen the note, warning Gaby not to "go down the same path" as Joe, whatever that meant. Could that man be the mysterious Gunther Grossmann? The person Matt had told her about? The one he had gone looking for after she had shown him the note?

Maybe she should take a ride past the Haverson place, up on Birch Hill. It was in the sprawling subdivision known as Woodson Lake Estates, on the border with Prescott, the town to the north of Woodson Falls. At least the roads in the Estates were easier to navigate in the summer than in the winter, when she'd last been up there. She wasn't quite sure what she was looking for, but felt certain she should make the trip.

Chapter 26

GABY DROVE INTO TOWN late Monday morning, Kat at her side. The dog hung her head out the window, enjoying the breeze created by the car's motion. Gaby had put off driving past the Haverson house until today, a weekday, when whoever lived there now was unlikely to be home. She wasn't ready for a confrontation with the new owner, especially if he proved to be the man who had attacked Joe.

Most people who had lived in Woodson Falls for any length of time knew old Mrs. Haverson when she was still alive. At Halloween, children swapped spooky stories featuring Sadie Haverson as a witch, daring each other to take their trick-or-treating to her house to see what might happen.

Gaby planned to stop at Mike's Place for a chat with her friend Emma before heading up to the Estates. Maybe Emma, who lived for gossip, could fill Gaby in on what was going on with the old house on Birch Hill.

"Hi, Emma," Gaby called, approaching the deli counter.

"Gaby! Nice to see you. It's been a while," Emma replied. "What'll you have?"

"How about a cinnamon-raisin bagel, lightly toasted, with no butter and a coffee?"

While Emma took care of the bagel, Gaby paid for her order, then poured her coffee from the urns next to the deli counter. She took the steaming cup to one of the tables in the small area set aside in Mike's Place for customers to eat their breakfast or lunch or simply hang out with a cup of coffee while chatting with a friend or reading the paper.

Emma joined her, plunking down the perfectly toasted bagel in front of her friend.

"What's going on?" she asked. "Any news on who did in old Pinkham?"

"Nothing yet," Gaby answered, sipping her coffee now that it had cooled off a bit. "The case is being handled at the state level based on any information the trooper or I can provide about Mr. Pinkham and possible suspects. Have you heard anything?"

"Not really. That Mutt-and-Jeff duo claiming to be Pinkham's friends from way back, I think their names are Adam and Bud, were in a few times. They were bragging to whoever would listen that Pinkham left them lots in the subdivision he was working on. I know you were Pinkham's lawyer. Will you be handling his estate?"

"Yes. He named me as executor, although that has to be approved by the court."

"Will you have to complete work on the subdivision and sell the rest of the lots?"

"Unfortunately, yes. It'll be a lot more complicated than the usual estate."

"Well, good luck with that."

Gaby bit into the bagel, still warm from the toaster. "Yum. Have a question for you."

"Shoot," said Emma, seeming to sense that questions often led to more gossip.

"Do you know anything about the Haverson place up on Birch Hill in the Estates?"

"Someone bought it from Sadie's estate a while back. I think they're planning to flip it. You aren't thinking of moving from your darling cottage, are you?"

"No, just curious about whoever bought it. You think it's a flip?"

"That's what I heard. I believe Robin Meyerson is the agent handling the sale."

"Oh, I know Robin. I was considering using her when the Sunrise Hills lots are ready for sale," Gaby said, finishing her bagel and continuing to sip her coffee.

"Here's one for the records," Emma said, not ready to return to the deli to handle the crowd that would be clamoring for sandwiches in less than an hour. "Did you hear that Nancy Beachum is closing up shop and moving to Florida? I haven't a clue where I'll go to have my hair done. It was so convenient to pop in down the street when I needed a trim."

"Nell mentioned it to me the other day."

"Well! Did Nell tell you that a newcomer to town—Myra Nichols—is planning to open a bookstore in that space? Thinking of calling it The Book Shelf! Crazy or what?" Emma exclaimed.

"I had the same reaction. Interesting name for a bookstore, though."

"But give me a break. A bookstore? In Woodson Falls?" Emma asked, getting up and retying her apron. "Better get back behind the counter. Great to see you, Gab. Stop in again—sooner this time."

"Will do. Thanks for the info on the house, Em," Gaby said, tossing her empty cup and paper plate into the trash.

Kat barked a greeting through the open window as Gaby approached her car. *Off to the Estates!*

It was a pleasant drive past Woodson Lake, the small state park on its shores packed with vacationers, even this early in the week.

July and August were busy months for Woodson Falls. Things would quiet down after Labor Day.

Gaby had consulted her town map before embarking on this adventure and had a vague idea of the location of Birch Hill, an offshoot of Bog Hollow in the tangle of narrow roads, mostly dirt, many unmarked, that characterized the Estates. She made her way up Pleasantview before encountering the gated entrance, closed during summer to prevent non-residents from intruding on the private lake community in search of less crowded beaches. She usually requested the code to the gate when she had a client who lived in the Estates, but the number had likely changed since the last time she was here.

Waiting patiently for a delivery truck to drive out so she could scoot through before the gate closed, she wondered what she expected to learn. Perhaps a look at the property would shake some memory loose or, more likely, give her an excuse to call Robin Meyerson in an attempt to learn who was selling it.

Gaby didn't have long to wait before a FedEx van came out so she could drive through the open gate, making her way to Bog Hollow. Her map had indicated that Birch Hill was the second left off Bog Hollow, so she took the turn when she encountered it, about a quarter-mile down the road. There was a single house on the short spur, a typical New England saltbox with a "For Sale" sign in front, just as Matt had told her. Though how anyone would see the sign without being directed to this particular property was anybody's guess.

The yard surrounding the house was heavily wooded. Gaby could see cuts in branches that had been trimmed back around the sides. The exterior of the building had been shingled recently. The telltale fresh wooden shingles hadn't had time to darken. The roof looked new as well, with none of the moss and lichen that were quick to appear when a building was in the shadow of many trees. A white picket fence added to the general appeal of the property, serving as an obvious sign of recent work to get the property in shape for a sale.

Reluctant to get any closer to the house in order to snoop, even though there was no evidence of anyone around, Gaby decided to look on one of the realty websites to see if she could find photos of any interior work that had been done.

Returning home, she fired up her computer and checked Zillow to see if she could locate houses on the market in town. A handful of Woodson Falls properties were listed, among them, the house on Birch Hill. The listing touted the recent renovation of the house, the privacy of the property, as well as the benefits of living in a gated community with access to several beaches.

While there were only a few shots of the house's interior, it was obvious that considerable work had been done, including a modern-looking kitchen and an up-to-date bath. The remaining rooms were bare of furniture or window treatments—a clean slate for a potential buyer. The property was listed at $359,999.

Gaby exited the site to find contact information for Robin Meyerson. She placed the call and was surprised to find the Realtor at her desk.

"Robin Meyerson. How may I help you?"

"My name is Gabriella Quinn. I'm an attorney here in Woodson Falls, and I'm curious about the listing on Birch Hill."

"Oh! That's such a special property!" the real estate agent exclaimed, moving straight into her sales pitch. "The house was built in the fifties, but it's structurally sound. A total rehab was completed recently. It's a beauty in a lovely gated community. But you know Woodson Lake Estates, I'm sure. Would you like me to arrange a showing? I'm available anytime this week."

"Actually, I'm curious about the seller or, more specifically, the individual or company that did the rehab on the property."

"The owner purchased the property about a year ago from the Haverson estate. Let me see… Ah, here. It's Gregor Garrison Associates, LLC. They handled the work on the property."

"Do you have contact information you could share with me?"

"May I ask what your interest is? I don't believe the owner would entertain a private sale when he's signed a listing agreement with us."

"Of course," Gaby answered, not wanting to discuss her interest in learning more about the individual who was likely the stranger responsible for the notes she had received. She knew that people using aliases often chose names similar to their real names. Gregor Garrison wasn't a far cry from Gunther Grossmann. "I understand. Thank you for talking with me. By the way, I was the attorney for the gentleman who was developing the Sunrise Hills subdivision. He passed away recently…"

"Was he the person who died in that awful explosion around the Fourth of July?"

"Yes. I'm probably going to be handling his estate, and I'll be looking for a real estate agent to manage the sale of the lots once they've been appraised and the road is put in. Would you be interested?"

"Of course! Please do contact me when you're ready. I probably can give you a discount on the commission given the number of lots to be marketed. But how is that related to the Birch Hill property?"

"It isn't. Well, thanks again for your help. I'll give you a call when I'm ready to move ahead with Sunrise Hills."

Chapter 27

THE PROBATE HEARING concerning Pinkham's estate was scheduled for August 17, a mere four weeks after Gaby had submitted the application to probate his will. That was a record time for the court, most likely because the people who had called Gaby were pestering the court with their claims. Most estates proceeded without the need for a hearing, but Gaby had been expecting one to be scheduled, just not this quickly. Not that it mattered. She was prepared to defend Pinkham's decisions, as expressed in the will she had drafted on his behalf.

The court's hearing room was located toward the rear of the space devoted to probate matters in the Prescott Town Hall, behind a larger office where staff worked. People attending a hearing or a meeting with the judge were required to sign in before being allowed to cross the office space and enter the hearing room or approach Judge Hiram Samuel Taylor's chambers, which were in a corner office, adjacent to both the hearing room and the central office space.

A large mahogany table dominated the room in which the hearing would take place. Gaby took a seat across from a young woman who introduced herself as Melissa Crowe, attorney for

Edith Vincent and Raymond Pinkham. Evidently, Ms. Vincent had taken Gaby's advice to retain local counsel to handle the cousins' challenge to the will. Both attorneys removed files from their briefcases, each setting them on the table along with a yellow legal pad and pen.

The chief clerk, Audrey Young, entered the room with a tape recorder, legal pad and pen. "All rise," she said as Judge Taylor left his office to take a seat at the head of the table.

After settling in his chair, the judge said, "Be seated." Turning to his clerk, he asked her to read the hearing notice.

After doing so, she announced, "Present are Attorney Gabriella Quinn, representing the estate, and Attorney Melissa Crowe of Springer, Evans, Strauss and Gerkin, representing Edith Vincent and Raymond Pinkham, heirs of the decedent, Winston Pinkham. Petitioners Adam Samuelson and Harold Wiseman have not yet arrived."

"Thank you," the judge nodded to the clerk. Turning to the two attorneys, he said, "Good morning. Before we begin, Attorney Crowe—doesn't Paul Evans usually represent your firm's clients on probate matters?"

"Yes, Your Honor," Crowe said, rising to speak. "Attorney Evans has taken a leave of absence from the firm to care for his father. I'm filling in for him on probate cases."

"Thank you. No need to stand. We're not that formal an operation here," the judge said with a smile. "Now, can you state your clients' concerns regarding the decedent's will?"

Having taken her seat, Crowe opened the file she had brought to the hearing and, referring to it, said, "Ms. Edith Vincent and Mr. Raymond Pinkham, cousins of the decedent, ask the court to set aside the document submitted for probate purporting to be the decedent's last will and testament Both and declare it void. They have reason to believe the decedent was incompetent to make the will presented to this court, and they further question the nomination of Attorney Quinn as executor of the estate."

"And the grounds for these concerns?"

"My clients assert that, because they are the decedent's sole surviving heirs, he surely would have left a more substantial portion of his estate to them than is reflected in the will submitted to the court, and that his failure to do so is evidence of his mental incapacity. Additionally, they consider it inappropriate for Attorney Quinn to serve as executor of the decedent's estate when relatives of the decedent are able and willing to serve in that role. They also contend that, as the attorney who drafted the decedent's will, Attorney Quinn has a conflict of interest in assuming the role of executor."

"Dealing with the first question of capacity, can you offer the court a physician's report in relation to the claim regarding the decedent's legal incapacity to make a will?" Judge Taylor asked.

"No, Your Honor."

"And is there any other basis to support this claim?"

"I'm afraid not, Your Honor."

"I assume you explained to your clients that the decedent was not required by law to provide anything to his relatives and that some evidence of his legal incapacity was necessary to set aside the will and declare that the decedent died intestate?"

"Yes, Your Honor, but they were insistent that I express their concerns to the court. They didn't want to go to the expense of requesting a written report from the decedent's physician."

"I see. Attorney Quinn, have you anything to offer on the question of capacity?"

"Not formally, Your Honor. I can testify that I worked with the decedent for many years and, in the course of my representation, drafted several successive wills on his behalf. Had I reason to be concerned Mr. Pinkham no longer had the legal capacity to execute the will presented to the court, I would have urged him to allow an earlier will to serve as an expression of his wishes.

"I also took the precaution, as I'm sure the court will note, to have the two witnesses to the will sign an affidavit addressing the issue of competency, along with other conditions surrounding the execution of the will. The witnesses to the will are available to testify in the matter if necessary."

"So noted. Now, turning to the decedent's nomination of Attorney Quinn as executor. Attorney Quinn, can you provide the court with any insight you might have into the decedent's decision with respect to the appointment of an executor?"

"Yes, Your Honor. Mr. Pinkham and I discussed this issue at length in the course of drafting his will. He had limited contact with his two cousins, despite their being his only surviving kin, and said he thought his financial affairs were too complicated to be managed from a distance by someone who had little insight into his thinking. Both cousins live out of state, one in Wisconsin and the other in Idaho.

"I did suggest to Mr. Pinkham that he consider nominating his accountant, with whom he had frequent contact and who had an understanding of his financial matters, to serve in the role of executor. Mr. Pinkham did approach him, but the accountant declined to act in this capacity. Mr. Pinkham then asked if I would accept the role given our ongoing relationship and my familiarity with his finances. As the court knows, it's not unusual for an elderly person with no close relatives to name his or her attorney as executor."

"And as to the question of conflict of interest?" the judge asked. He turned to Attorney Crowe and said, "I'm assuming by 'conflict of interest' your clients are claiming Attorney Quinn coerced the decedent to name her as executor?"

"Yes, Your Honor," Crowe replied, her cheeks reddening in apparent embarrassment at having to assert her clients' claims without any supporting evidence.

"Attorney Quinn?" asked the judge, turning to address Gaby.

"I suggested to Mr. Pinkham that he identify two individuals to serve as witnesses to his execution of the will as required by statute," Gaby began. "He spoke with people at the bank he used in Westbury and arranged to have two tellers serve as witnesses. Because Mr. Pinkham no longer drove, I brought him there when the will was ready for signature. The bank personnel had reserved a room in which real estate closings often occur and also provided a notary public to officiate at the will's execution and administer the oath contained in the affidavit accompanying the will. I remained outside the room while the will was executed by Mr. Pinkham to eliminate any suggestion that I influenced his decisions as expressed in the will."

"Thank you, Attorney Quinn. Do you have anything else to offer on this matter, Attorney Crowe?"

"No, Your Honor," Crowe responded with a weak smile.

"Very well. Having heard the evidence—and I use the term lightly in this instance—from Attorney Crowe on behalf of the individuals challenging the will, I am ready to rule on both the matter of the legal capacity of the decedent as well as on the issue of conflict of interest regarding the decedent's nomination of Attorney Quinn as executor.

"There being no compelling evidence to the contrary, I find that the decedent, Winston Pinkham, had the legal capacity to make the will presented to the court. The fact that the decedent named his sole surviving heirs as beneficiaries under the will, regardless of the size of their share in his estate, suggests that his memory was intact. There is no legal requirement that a decedent provide for his relatives or even his issue, the sole exception being the provision for a spouse, which doesn't apply in this case, the decedent having never married according to the application to probate his will.

"As to the issue of the appointment of an executor and the potential conflict of interest in having Attorney Quinn fill this role, I find that sufficient precautions were taken to avoid even the appearance of conflict of interest and that the decedent's decision in this regard was a reasonable one.

"Therefore, the court admits the Last Will and Testament of Winston Pinkham dated April 10, 2022, to probate and appoints Gabriella Quinn as executor of said estate, effective this date, August 17, 2022. So ordered." Turning to his clerk, he added, "You'll prepare the decree and notices for my signature?"

"Of course, Your Honor."

"Then this hearing is adjourned."

"Excuse me, Your Honor," Young piped up. "We were expecting two additional petitioners. Shall I see if they've arrived?"

"Don't bother," Taylor said, getting up to head to his chambers. "If they couldn't get here while the hearing was in progress, I don't see much point in continuing this matter."

Chapter 28

Gaby and Melissa left the town hall together.

"Well, that was embarrassing!" Melissa exclaimed.

"I can't imagine it was any fun, but you have to do what your client wants, even when you know it's not going to get them anywhere."

"I know, but I've never appeared before this judge—or any judge, for that matter. And now I hope I never need to be in a court again. That whole scene made me feel so incompetent, even though you're right. I had no choice given my clients' strong directive."

"You really shouldn't worry too much about it. It'll be hard giving your clients the news, but I'm sure you already told them it would be an uphill battle. It's not easy to get a will tossed out without a pile of strong evidence proving the testator's incompetence."

"Still, that was brutal."

"How long have you been practicing?" Gaby asked. She'd never run into Melissa in the course of another case, nor seen her at a bar event.

"I graduated last May and was admitted to the Connecticut bar in August. Landed the job at Springer Evans in October, probably only because Attorney Evans was going on extended leave."

"Believe me when I say it takes time to develop the personal fortitude not to take events like today personally. If you're doing your job in terms of knowing the law related to the matter you're involved with, prepping your clients for a possible negative conclusion—even if you're convinced you'll win—and following the Rules of Professional Conduct, you'll be fine."

"Thanks for that. Everyone at Springer Evans has been nice, but they're all so busy with other matters there certainly hasn't been any mentoring going on. But maybe that's too much to expect."

"I never practiced in a firm, so I'm not sure how that works. My legal mentor is a retired lawyer in Woodson Falls. It does help a lot to have someone to bounce things off. Please feel free to call me if you have any questions."

"I will. It's been great to meet you, Attorney Quinn."

"It's Gaby, and nice to meet you as well," Gaby said, accepting Melissa's proffered hand.

"Hope I run into you again," Melissa said, turning up the street in the other direction, "Just not in court."

"Be well," Gaby called, turning to walk to her car. Deep in thought about the trials and tribulations faced by any young attorney starting out, herself included, she didn't notice the two men approaching her.

"Well, if it ain't Attorney Quinn," said the tall one she recognized as Adam Samuelson. "Aren't you headed the wrong way? Prescott Town Hall is behind you."

"Excuse me?"

"The hearing on old Pinky's will. Don't you have to be there?" the shorter man, Bud Wiseman, asked.

"I think you boys missed the boat," Gaby replied. "The hearing is over."

"Huh?" the two grunted at the same time.

"Why don't you go up to the probate office? If the judge is in a good mood, maybe he'll listen to your claim," Gaby suggested, knowing that Judge Taylor was more likely to read them the riot act for not showing up to the hearing on time as well as dismiss their claim.

The men headed to the town hall, and Gaby continued toward her car. She was eager to begin the next phase of administering Pinkham's estate, knowing that this crucial hearing was behind her and she could move ahead confidently now that the court had validated Pinkham's choice of executor.

Gaby skipped her planned lunch at the Greene Bean in favor of having something at home. She wanted to dive into the estate administration steps she'd outlined while waiting for the results of the probate hearing. Putting her briefcase back in her office, she went out with Kat for a bit of fresh air and a game of fetch, giving the dog some exercise and herself a needed break to clear her head.

Returning to the cottage with Kat panting at her side, she refilled the dog's water bowl, grabbed a protein bar and a couple of plums, and headed back to the room she used as an office. It was only then that she noticed the flashing light signaling a phone message.

Pressing the playback button, she heard Matt's voice. "Hi, Gaby. Hope today's hearing went well. Give me a call when you can? I heard back from the detective at Major Crimes."

She dialed Matt's office number, wondering whether the detective Matt had heard from was working the Pinkham case or her own incident. After several rings, the call was routed to the barracks, where she was invited to leave a message for the trooper.

"Gabriella Quinn returning Officer Thomas's call. I'll be in my office for the rest of the day." Giving the dispatcher her number, she hung up. Although she had Matt's cell number, she decided not to try him on it. His absence from the office meant he likely was tied up in some police business or, possibly, taking a lunch break at the café. Regardless, his message didn't have a note of urgency to it, so she pushed thoughts about the trooper aside to focus on putting into motion her plan for the many threads to be followed in administering Pinkham's estate.

Her first call was to a company specializing in cleaning up properties following a fire. She explained her decision to leave the foundation of 2 Sunrise Trail intact if it was salvageable. Anyone building on the lot would have to keep within the original footprint of the house. A new structure would be required to meet zoning requirements regarding setbacks from the road and lot boundaries unless a zoning variance was granted. Leaving the foundation of Pinkham's house might lower the value of the property in terms of a sale, but would provide a more valuable guide to a potential buyer since the structure had been built many years ago, prior to Woodson Falls' creation of zoning regulations. On the other hand, depending on its condition, having an intact foundation might increase the lot's value, as the buyer wouldn't have to do this work.

Thinking about Sunrise Trail led to her next call—to an appraiser she had used in the past. Given the cost of appraising properties, she had waited until she was formally appointed executor before asking the appraiser to determine the value of each lot in the Sunrise Hills subdivision as well as the lot at 2 Sunrise Trail. This information would be reported on the Connecticut probate court's Form PC-440, the inventory of estate assets. The appraisal also would guide the pricing of the lots by a Realtor. There was little buildable land remaining in Woodson Falls, which would enhance the value of these lots. Most of the town's remaining vacant land was under conservation or abutted wetlands, which usually deemed it unbuildable.

Gaby thought it would be prudent to have the subdivision road and related drainage system constructed before the lots were placed on the market. Doing so would further enhance the value of the lots. She had a list of contractors from whom she would request bids to do the work. She would have to talk with the engineer at Blackberry Hill Engineering, which had been responsible for the subdivision planning, to ask that the firm develop specifications for the road work.

The clearing of the property at 2 Sunrise Trail, the appraisal of the subdivision lots, and the construction of the subdivision road would all cost money, so her next step would be to transfer all of Pinkham's financial assets into an estate account. She would need fiduciary certificates issued by the probate court to allow her to act with respect to estate assets. Those certificates as well as a decree admitting the will to probate and identifying Gaby as the executor would come from the court in a few days, now that the hearing had been held.

In the meantime, she could go to the Internal Revenue Service's website to apply for a tax identification number, or EIN, for the estate. This number, equivalent to an individual's social security number, was required for such entities as businesses, charitable organizations, trusts and estates.

Gaby worked steadily through the afternoon, achieving all she had set out to do. Ready for a break and some dinner, she was startled when the phone rang. She'd completely forgotten about Matt's earlier call.

"Law offices, Gabriella…"

"It's me, Gaby," Matt said. "Got a few minutes? I heard from the detective Major Crimes assigned to the Pinkham murder and arson. His name is Nathan Irving."

"Absolutely! I'm all ears."

"Detective Irving was able to contact all three of Pinkham's New York visitors. Turns out they had worked with him years ago in the banking industry when he lived in the city. Anyway, they said they left Woodson Falls around eleven in the morning, following their breakfast with Pinkham at the café. When they took Pinkham back to Sunrise Trail, they settled him in his usual chair and switched his oxygen tubing from the portable oxygen concentrator to the larger unit. They turned the machine on but didn't look at the setting. Pinkham said it was already at the right level.

"They thought Pinkham looked a bit fatigued after being out to breakfast, but said he was grateful they had come and had enjoyed their visit. Apparently the men try to see Pinkham twice a year, once around Thanksgiving and the other time around the Fourth of July, when the New York friends have a bit of time. Said he was their 'rabbi' when they began in the banking industry and they were eternally grateful to him for paving the way to their success."

"Hmm… Well, at least you have a time for when someone last saw Pinkham. That helps, doesn't it?" Gaby asked.

"It does, but there's more."

Chapter 29

"MORE?" Gaby asked.

"Have you had supper?" Matt replied.

"No, not yet. Why?"

"Want to meet at the café? Go over what I learned?"

Gaby chuckled. "We're together there so often, people will talk."

"Do you mind?"

"No, do you?"

"Not in the least."

"I'll be there in a bit. I need to feed Kat and change."

"I've got a ton of paperwork to go through, but I'll be over there as soon as I can."

Gaby showered, changed back into the slacks and blouse she'd worn to court, then fed Kat before heading to the town center and the Sunshine Café.

Matt hadn't yet arrived, so Gaby slipped into a booth and ordered an iced tea. She smiled as she thought about Pinkham's apparent practice of taking people under his wing, even though that sometimes led to his association with the likes of Adam and Bud.

She was happy to learn his New York friends had stayed in touch, visiting regularly, grateful for his support and guidance in their careers. She wondered what their names were. There were a few New Yorkers among Pinkham's many beneficiaries. Had Pinkham remembered any of these visitors in his will, and would that offer a motive for his murder? She'd have to add that to the discussion with Matt.

When the trooper arrived some fifteen minutes later, he ordered a coffee and said, "Thanks for coming out. Detective Irving got a lot of information from Pinkham's visitors, and it's easier for me to tell you about it in person rather than over the phone."

"No problem," Gaby responded with a smile. "Always happy to see you."

Suzie, the young waitress who had served them before, came to their booth to take their order.

"What'll it be, folks?" she asked, no longer as flirty as she'd been before, most likely sensing that Gaby and Matt just might be a couple.

"I'll have the chicken salad special, please," Gaby said.

"Mom's meatloaf and mashed potatoes for me, Suzie," Matt said with a smile, handing their menus back to the waitress.

"Before you tell me what else you learned," Gaby said, after Suzie had left. "Is there any chance one of the New Yorkers killed Pinkham and set up the explosion for long after they were gone?"

"Well, they alibi each other, and then there's the question of motive. Irving didn't think they were involved. All of them would have had to be in on it, and Irving thought that unlikely." Matt looked down at his notes and read off their names. "Were any of them beneficiaries of Pinkham's will?"

"Nothing rings a bell, but I'll check. I was wondering about that myself. So what else did you learn?" Gaby asked.

"One of the men the New York detectives spoke with reported seeing a middle-aged man coming up the walk as they were leaving Pinkham's house and getting into their car. He greeted them with a wave, but didn't state his name or his purpose for visiting Pinkham on a Sunday. It seemed to them like he was probably a frequent visitor of Pinkham's so they didn't think much of it. And while he's pretty sure the individual drove to Sunrise Trail, he didn't remember anything about his car.

"He said Pinkham himself hadn't mentioned he was expecting anyone. And he hadn't expressed any urgency to return home after breakfast, as if he expected a visitor later that morning. In fact, this individual thought Pinkham would have lingered at the café a bit longer despite his obvious fatigue, but the men were eager to beat the holiday weekend traffic they expected on their drive back to the city.

"Irving promised to send me a copy of the written reports of his interviews with the New York gentlemen, but wanted me to know when they last saw Pinkham to help pin down the time of death."

"Interesting," Gaby commented, wondering who this new visitor might be.

Suzie arrived with their meals and offered to refill their beverages. After she'd given Gaby a fresh iced tea and poured more coffee into Matt's mug, Gaby asked, "Did the person who mentioned the later visitor describe the man they saw approach Pinkham's house?"

"According to Irving, he described the person as shorter than average—maybe five-two—but well built, muscular. Balding, suntanned. In his late fifties or early sixties. Carrying a briefcase. Dressed casually. Does that sound like anyone we've been talking about?"

"I ran into Adam and Bud when I came out of the hearing, so they're fresh in my mind," Gaby answered. "Adam is tall, slim, full head of longish brown hair. Bud is shorter than average, about five-four, I'd say, and portly. Certainly not well built or muscular. And he has a head of very curly black hair."

"What about Conway?"

"I've never met him," Gaby said with a shake of her head. "Just talked with him on the phone. What else did you learn?"

"The information we have from what appears to be the last people to see Pinkham alive, other than the murderer or murderers, tells us he was alive and well until at least eleven that Sunday morning. I asked Brian, the fire marshal, how long it would take for enough gas to accumulate to lead to the explosion. The explosion occurred at about nine-thirty on the night of the parade and fireworks. Given the size of the cut in the gas line into the house as well as its location and the high level of oxygen flowing from the concentrator, Brian thought Pinkham could have been killed anytime after eleven since his death wasn't caused by the explosion.

"He contacted the telephone company to trace the origin of the call, but it had been made from a burner phone, so he wasn't able to trace it.

"Because it was most likely a telephone call that triggered the explosion, once the perp killed Pinkham, he might have just waited to set it off, possibly timing it to coincide with the fireworks. It's likely the explosion was intended to cover up any evidence that would lead to the murderer."

"Wasn't that a bit risky? Waiting? Anyone might have come to visit Pinkham between the time he was murdered and the explosion."

"Good point, but we do know no one reported finding Pinkham dead and covered with blood, so if it was a risk, it paid off."

"Okay, but how do you catch a criminal if there's no evidence available to tie a person to a crime?" Gaby asked. "How do you even know where to start, what to look for? I know it's hard to convict someone for murder without a body. I'm not sure how you would do it without a shred of evidence."

"It'll be difficult, but the first step is to narrow down the field of suspects. Once we've done that, we look to motive, means and opportunity. The killer or killers are likely to benefit in some way by Pinkham's death. They had to have knowledge regarding how gas explosions occur and what sets them off. There's minimal skill involved in setting that up, and it doesn't require special tools. The element of opportunity is best determined through the alibis suspects provide. We can assume Pinkham knew his killer since he let the person into the house."

"I'm not so sure of that. While I agree Pinkham's murderer probably was someone he knew, we can't rule out the possibility of a stranger. Pinkham never locked his door," Gaby ventured.

"What?" Matt exclaimed. "In this day and age? With all the notices I put in the local paper warning residents to keep their homes and vehicles locked?"

"I've found that old-timers seldom consider themselves at risk," Gaby answered with a smile. "Old habits die hard. Older ones are even harder to break. I always knocked before I came in to let Win know I had arrived, but anyone could waltz into the house."

"I'd still want to pursue this under the assumption Pinkham knew his killer. The whole scene is too elaborate, too organized for a random robber. The strength behind the blow to the neck—sufficient to nick the vertebrae—the probable heft of the knife or other sharp weapon—heavy enough to inflict such a substantial wound and not likely to be something that was lying around the house—plus the effort behind the explosion. Whoever did this had to know Pinkham used propane as well as oxygen, and that he still owned a landline. This was an organized murder, not some random attack."

"Okay," Gaby said, nodding. "So, where does that take us?"

"Back to the list we discussed before, I guess," Matt said, nearly done with his dinner and ready for dessert, while Gaby had eaten only half her salad.

"Can I throw in something that's been bugging me?"

"Sure," Matt responded, mopping up the last of his gravy with a roll.

"Is there any way Win's murder might be connected to the dead cat on my doorstep and the note on my door? A lot of people knew Win was my client, and one I was fond of. After all, two different detectives are involved in these investigations, Irving on the arson and Pinkham's murder, and Fisher on the note and the dead cat. And then there's Joe's murder. Maybe all these cases are connected, and no one's been able to pull them together."

Matt smiled, "Highly unlikely, I would think," Matt answered, smiling. "I know you're anxious to get answers to that, but let's tuck your question into the back of our minds. If we can connect the dots once we know who killed Pinkham, fine. But I think it's a dead end in terms of this crime."

Chapter 30

Matt ordered a slice of Boston cream pie. Gaby asked for an oatmeal raisin cookie.

"So, back to the list of potential suspects we discussed a while back?" Gaby started.

"Let's start with the unlikely ones and why you don't think any of them killed Pinkham," Matt replied. "I have my own thoughts, but you were closest to the man and his situation. Plus, you've got great intuition."

"Hmm... Sometimes," Gaby replied with a smile. "Okay, I'd rule out his accountant, his bookkeeper, the housekeeper-shopper, and any of the many drivers who took him to medical appointments. None are mentioned in the will or have any interest in Win's estate. In fact, other than the drivers, all would be losing a paying client if he died."

"Agreed," Matt said, taking a forkful of pie.

"The two cousins seem far-fetched. Five hundred dollars is hardly enough to prompt a murder, even though they mounted a halfhearted effort to challenge the will at the probate hearing earlier today. Did Detective Irving check them out to verify they were each in their respective states the day Win was killed?"

"He did. Neither had traveled in quite a while, and one is still recovering from hip replacement surgery," Matt replied, "so we can forget them. Who else?"

"Well, I guess the visitors from New York need to be ruled out. I'll double-check when I get home, but I'm pretty sure none of them are mentioned in the will. From what Detective Irving told you, it's highly unlikely they are involved," Gaby ventured. "Other than accelerating a bequest or stopping the development of Sunrise Hills, I can't think of a motive for killing an old man who was likely to die in a few years anyway."

"Agreed."

"I mentioned the people Win dealt with at Blackberry Hill Engineering in connection with the Sunrise Hills subdivision. Although they may have prolonged the subdivision approval process, costing Pinkham a good deal in fees, there's no good reason for any of them to want him dead. In fact, it was more likely he'd be turning to them again to design the road and drainage system, something I'm going to have to do."

"Okay. Does that bring us back to this Conway fellow and the Adam and Bud duo as the main viable suspects?"

"I guess so, but why don't I give you a list of the beneficiaries identified in Win's will? It's public knowledge anyway, now that the will's been accepted by the probate court. You could pass it on to Detective Irving. He might want to cover all bases and check the alibis of each of the people with an interest in Win's estate. Although, again, I can't see anyone murdering him just to receive a bequest sooner."

"Probably a good idea," Matt responded, smiling at her. "You have a real knack for this. Sure you don't want to go into police work?"

"Totally sure, as I've told you before. I much prefer the 'law' side of things," Gaby replied, answering his smile.

Suzie brought their check and cleared their plates. "No rush on that. Slow night," she said, leaving the two to continue their conversation.

"So, of the three—Samuelson, Wiseman and Conway—who do you think 'dunnit'?" Matt mused.

"I just don't know," Gaby answered as her mind ranged over what she knew about the three.

"Let's start with Samuelson and Wiseman," Matt said, encouraging Gaby to provide any details she might have on the pair, especially since she had seen them in Prescott for the probate hearing earlier in the day.

"Well, even though I still have doubts either of those gentlemen could pull off a complex scenario like the explosion, their ill-founded conviction that Win intended to give each of them their selected subdivision lot outright might just be a motive to kill him, especially if—as I suspect—neither has sufficient funds to purchase the lots, even at a discount."

"You said a while back that the court was unlikely to accept the letter from Pinkham they claimed gave them the lots outright, didn't you?"

"Yup. At the very least, any change in the language of the will or Win's intentions would have had to be formalized in a codicil to his will. He was thinking about adding one that donated the land to the land trust if he died before the road was put in, but he never acted on the thought. And, as I said before, I doubt Pinkham wrote such a letter, but it wouldn't matter to the court even if he had."

"Is that what happened at the hearing?"

"Funny thing is, Samuelson and Wiseman never made it there. They were expected, but came so late the hearing was completed and the judge had admitted the will to probate and accepted Win's nomination of me as executor before they even arrived!"

"I did some digging on them, as well as on Conway," Matt reported. "Samuelson and Wiseman both moved to the area from Queens. They rent an apartment together in Prescott. Neither ever married. Both finished high school, no college. Samuelson works as a driver with UPS. Wiseman works at the Staples store in Prescott. They apparently landed in this area after Pinkham brought them up from the city on weekends to work on land trust properties, just like Peggy mentioned he did with many others too. And both joined the Prescott Volunteer Fire Department when they arrived up here, likely at Pinkham's urging to get involved with the community. They completed the basic training as entry-level firefighters and served for a few years. Wiseman dropped out while Samuelson continues to volunteer, but that means…"

"They actually just might have the knowledge and skills to pull off a gas explosion!" Gaby exclaimed. "Wow! Interesting! I thought I spotted Adam in firefighter gear at the site of the Win's house, but I was so distressed by the probability that Win was dead I wasn't sure."

"Happens," Matt said softly, "even to those of us who are trained to put such feelings aside. It's hard, especially if you're familiar with the victim."

"I guess so," Gaby responded. "You said you also did some digging on Conway?"

"I ran a background check on him, as I did with Samuelson and Wiseman. Conway moved to Woodson Falls from Pennsylvania following his divorce. No children. He worked for a fuel oil company there, in their scheduling department. The company sold and installed heating and air-conditioning equipment as well as delivering residential heating oil and propane. They also provided maintenance for heating and air-conditioning units. Apparently Conway left the company on good terms. The individual I talked to said he was a steady worker and reliable but had 'sub-optimal' interpersonal skills that kept him from being promoted to a managerial position."

"Did the person you talked to elaborate any on what he meant by 'sub-optimal interpersonal skills'? That might well explain how boorish he can be."

"No, even though I asked. I had told him I was doing an informal background check for a company in the area that was considering Conway for a vacant position."

"That makes sense. So, Conway might have a passing familiarity with propane and maybe even some sense of the dangers if a leak occurred. Or maybe not."

Matt continued. "I made a point of visiting the land trust office to meet him. He looks a bit like the person Pinkham's New York visitors saw as they were leaving, but eyewitness descriptions are notoriously inaccurate. Even if the visitor they saw was Conway, it still doesn't make him the murderer. He might have had a legitimate reason to visit Pinkham that morning, such as land trust business. And it's entirely possible that the murderer came to the house later in the day. Unfortunately, with Pinkham's house tucked into the woods and down the road and no other homes on Sunrise Trail, it's impossible to canvas the area to see if a neighbor saw anything."

"Did you ask Conway whether he called on Win that day?" Gaby asked.

"No, I didn't want to ask him anything about Pinkham that might give him time to create an alibi or destroy evidence if he was the killer. I made some excuse about wanting to get to know people involved with organizations in town."

"Hmm... Interesting," Gaby said. "Still, even though I took an instant dislike to Conway and my further dealings with him have done nothing to change my opinion of the man, I just don't see what motive he might have for killing Win. He didn't seem to know about the charitable remainder trust, which will go to the land trust in any event, not to him personally. He assumed Win left a substantial bequest to the trust through his will and was disappointed that he hadn't, but such a bequest wouldn't have benefited Conway either.

"He had his eye on the Sunrise Hills property Win was developing and wanted him to donate it to the land trust, but Win had refused his request on several occasions. I don't think he knew Win had considered executing a codicil to his will, favoring the land trust. Conway even asked me to transfer the property to the trust as a charitable donation following Win's death, rather than proceed with the subdivision. All of that points to someone who is dedicated to land preservation in Woodson Falls—even zealous to the point of being obnoxious—but none of it feels like a motive for murder other than to feed his ego."

"Agreed. Possible motives that can be attributed to any of those three—Samuelson, Wiseman or Conway—are skimpy at best, but they're still the prime suspects."

"Now what?" Gaby asked.

"Now I think it would be best if I give all of this information to Detective Irving and see if he wants us to dig any further. You'll call me in the morning with everything you've suggested I convey to him?"

"Of course. And I'll pick up this check," Gaby said, pulling the bill over and opening her purse to pay. "And still invite you to dinner one of these days."

Matt smiled his thanks.

"Hmm…" Gaby got up from the booth. "Think I'll call the land trust office tomorrow and make an appointment to speak with Hilda Morrow, the part-time secretary. I need to talk with her anyway to see if the land trust is planning a memorial for Win. Maybe I can get her to chat a bit about Conway."

Chapter 31

GABY CALLED the land trust office the following morning, expecting to leave a message on a machine. Instead, a weary-sounding Hilda Morrow picked up.

"Good morning. Woodson Falls Land Trust. Hilda Morrow speaking," she announced.

"Good morning! I didn't expect to find anyone in the office on a Friday! Took a chance. My name is Gabriella Quinn. I'm an attorney here in Woodson Falls, and I'm handling the estate of Winston Pinkham, one of your longtime volunteers and officers."

"Of course! Win Pinkham. What a lovely man! We were all so shocked to learn he'd been murdered."

"Me too. It's so sad. He may have been old, but he still had a few good years ahead of him," Gaby replied. "People have been asking me about a memorial tribute or something similar to mark Mr. Pinkham's passing, and I've been wondering whether the land trust was planning such an event."

"I'm so glad you asked," Morrow responded with a sigh that sounded relieved. "I've been fielding calls from lots of folks asking the same thing. At this point, nothing's been planned, but I'd be happy to talk with you about arranging such an event."

"That would be wonderful," Gaby answered, wondering why the land trust hadn't acted on this itself. "Can I make an appointment to come in and discuss this with you? Perhaps sometime next week?"

"Do you have time today? We're usually slow on Fridays."

"I was planning to work from home today, so yes, I could come down to the office. What time would be good for you?"

"How about after lunch? Say, one or one-thirty?"

"Perfect. See you then."

The Woodson Falls Land Trust was housed in a lean-to shed attached to one of the buildings owned by the Woodson Falls Historical Society near the town center. In Woodson Falls' earliest days, the structure had housed a carriage shop that made plow handles and coffins in addition to horse-drawn carriages. The building later served as the town's post office.

Most recently, the historical society office had been located there, later to move to the loft space above the earliest store in town, now a gift shop owned and operated by the historical society. When they vacated their office across the road, the land trust quickly put in a bid to rent the space for its own operation. A small shed attached to the structure was used to store equipment for maintaining the trails on land trust properties.

The simple room housed two substantial desks, several filing cabinets, and a large surface on which was pinned a survey labeled "Meadow Ridge." Maps of the town with small flags marking land trust properties were hung from the walls along with photographs of various trails and viewpoints. Plastic display boxes positioned on the corner of the front desk were filled with pamphlets about the land trust and its properties, along with others identifying the location of the hiking trails maintained by the trust.

Morrow occupied the desk closest to the entrance, the doorframe low enough to require Gaby to duck when she entered. In her early sixties, Morrow wore her mostly grey hair in a bun on top of her head. Her gold-framed glasses perched on an upturned nose magnified a pair of twinkling blue eyes. She smiled broadly as she rose to greet Gaby.

"So pleased to meet you. Please, call me Hilda. Win had so many wonderful things to say about you," she said, adding, "I'm so relieved to have someone outside the land trust family ask about a memorial for dear Win."

"Oh?" Gaby responded, taking the chair next to Hilda's desk.

"Things have been a bit tense around here, everyone feeling like they have to tread lightly around Mr. Conway, the executive director, who is most decidedly against an event highlighting Win's contributions to the land trust."

"Why might that be?"

"Anyone's guess. Those two were at loggerheads since Mr. Conway came on board, yet it was Win's work that made the land trust such a successful, if small, conservation entity."

"Really?" Gaby said, indicating her interest in whatever the woman had to tell her. Hilda seemed to be bursting with information she longed to convey.

"Win was a true conservationist. He envisioned the land trust as providing an opportunity to preserve significant land in Woodson Falls, but he felt strongly about the land trust being prudent about its acquisitions."

"In what way?"

"He felt the land trust's acquisitions should be guided by the principles of contiguity, to preserve habitat corridors. That meant forgoing the acquisition of smaller properties dotted around the town that weren't connected to more substantial acres of conserved land.

"And he believed the land trust shouldn't bite off more than it could chew. It takes both people—usually volunteers—and funds to monitor and maintain conserved properties. Win felt acquiring land for the sake of acquiring land was foolish if the trust lacked the wherewithal to protect and support the properties it owns.

"I think that's one of the reasons he went ahead with his plans for the Sunrise Hills subdivision. While he claimed he was doing it to ensure he had sufficient funds to last him the rest of his life, he told me he didn't think that property, which was far removed from other open space, was worth the cost to the land trust of monitoring it."

"And Mr. Conway?"

"Just the opposite. The man's grabbing at every scrap of open space in Woodson Falls. All willy-nilly, without any guiding principles or concern for how we would maintain those properties. Some folks have complained that he's badgered them so much they've decided not to support the land trust at all anymore, which does significant damage to achieving our mission."

"Hmm… I've been a victim of a bit of his badgering, and I think Mr. Pinkham was as well. But what's Conway's goal, knowing that funding and manpower might not be able to support an explosion in the amount of acreage under trust control?"

"Well, between you and me, I voiced my own concerns to Conway one day when he seemed to be in a better mood than his usual churlishness. He said he hoped eventually to approach other small land trusts in this corner of the state to pool resources. Thought doing so would increase the number of volunteers as well as funds. And if the Woodson Falls Land Trust had more land under conservation than any of those other land trusts, he believed it was likely he'd be hired as a full-time executive director of the merged trust, at a larger salary than we can afford to pay. Of course, I have my doubts, given his total lack of people skills. But it seemed something he aspired to.

"He's also been talking about replacing the current board with people who agree with him on merging the WFLT with other small trusts. I know Win was in touch with most of the current board members to express his opposition to such a plan. I'm not sure what will happen now that he's died. His was the strongest voice, and he had a broad following within the land trust family. I just hope the board stays true to his values."

"Doesn't the trust have bylaws governing how board members are selected and replaced? I know from your mailings that it is a qualified charity under the IRS regulations, so there must be formal operating documents," Gaby offered. "I'm sure Conway can't act on his own authority to change the composition of the board."

"You're right! We could use a mind like yours on the board. I don't think Mr. Conway's ever even asked about those documents. Just bullies his way around the place." Hilda paused. "I probably shouldn't be saying this, but Conway has a temper. People are afraid to get on his wrong side. Challenging his desire to change the composition of the board may be an uphill battle."

"Well, regardless, as a legal entity, there are rules that can be asserted to counter his moves if the majority of sitting board members wishes to keep the trust local."

"Thanks! I'll pass that on to the chairman of the board. Provide some ammunition for the inevitable fight with Conway." Hilda made a note, then added, "Sorry to have gone on such a rant about land trust operations. Guess we'll just have to see what the future holds."

"Have you been with the land trust long?"

"I was a volunteer with the trust the first year my husband and I moved here, some forty-odd years ago. I continued to volunteer until I retired early from my teaching career, when I took this part-time position. Since then, I've been juggling secretarial duties along with membership campaigns and planning member activities and special events."

"Sounds like a full-time job to me."

"It can be, but that's my fault. It was a distraction after my husband died, and I guess I let my responsibilities with the trust morph into what I do today. Still, it's been satisfying in its own way, being the face, so to speak, of the trust. At least it was satisfying until Mr. Conway came on board and bullied his way into the executive director position when the person in that role had a heart attack and died suddenly. In fact, it's my involvement with planning special events that led to people asking me when something would be organized to recognize Win's longtime affiliation with the land trust.

"Enough about me and my issues. What did you have in mind for a memorial for Win?"

"I really haven't given it much thought, to tell you the truth. I guess I assumed the land trust would be doing something. But, with what you told me, I'm thinking that a picnic on one of the land trust properties might be a place to start. That would allow people to enjoy one of the locations the trust has conserved as well as share remembrances of Mr. Pinkham with others. I somehow think he would frown on anything very formal. Better to focus on celebrating his life and his contributions to the town through his involvement with the land trust rather than on mourning his death."

"I like that idea," Morrow responded. "There's a gorgeous piece of property—one of the first acquisitions by the trust. It's on a hilltop and has beautiful views. Probably best to plan something on a weekend a few weeks after Labor Day, when people are back in town from vacations. We could either set a rain date or, better, if it rains, move the picnic to one of the private community clubhouses we've used for events in the past."

"The estate could bear the cost of hamburgers, franks, buns and all the fixings. Do you think people might contribute starters, salads and desserts?"

"I'm certain people would be more than willing to help in that way," Hilda said.

"It'd be nice to have some tribute to Mr. Pinkham that participants could be involved in, something more than the usual eulogy," Gaby added. "When my sister died, we used flying wish paper to express our memories and thoughts, but because the wish papers involve fire, that's best done outdoors. If we don't have to move indoors, that might be a way people could honor Pinkham's memory."

"How about wildflower seed paper? That could work whether we're outside or indoors. People could write remembrances on slips of paper and let those thoughts eventually create a meadow in Win's memory. We could have some volunteers—many of whom Win recruited—plant the papers when the weather clears if we need to hold the event indoors."

"That would be lovely," Gaby said, getting up to leave and shaking Hilda's hand. "Thanks so much for meeting with me. Let me know how I can help with moving this forward."

She had her hand on the door to leave when a short, muscular man barreled through, nearly knocking her over.

Chapter 32

THE TAN, BALDING MAN who had almost run into her stepped back, eyeing her appraisingly. Gaby felt her skin crawl as his eyes ran from the top of her head down to her knees, then back again.

"Ho, ho, ho!" he exclaimed. "And who have we here? A new volunteer eager to join the WFLT? No paid positions available, of course, but plenty of room for a newcomer!"

Hilda had shot up from her desk as soon as the man opened the door. "Oh! Mr. Conway! I didn't expect you in today!" She was clearly ruffled by the man's sudden appearance in the small office. "This is Attorney Gabriella Quinn, Mr. Pinkham's attorney and the executor of his estate. Gaby? Please meet our executive director, Val Conway."

Although she was reluctant to do so, Gaby thrust her hand in the direction of the man standing no more than half a foot away, much too close for comfort. "We've talked on the phone, Mr. Conway. Glad to meet you in person," Gaby said, forcing a smile.

Ignoring Gaby's hand, Conway turned to Hilda and said, "I need the room, Ms. Morrow. Take the rest of the day off."

"Very well, Mr. Conway," Hilda responded, gathering her belongings and shimmying past Gaby and Conway as they remained standing just inside the office, staring at each other. "Great to meet you, Gaby," she whispered as she passed. "Have a good weekend. I'll be in touch."

After she had left, quietly closing the door behind her, Conway pointed to the chair next to the desk at the back of the room, silently directing Gaby to take a seat.

"And just what will our Ms. Morrow be in touch with you about?" he asked once he was seated in the wheeled executive's chair behind the desk. He glared at Gaby as he leaned back in the chair, arms folded across his chest.

"We were discussing having some type of memorial tribute for Mr. Pinkham. I had assumed the land trust would be planning something, given his long involvement with the group, and was offering my help, since his estate can pick up some of the costs. I was surprised to learn nothing had been arranged. Hilda and I sketched out some possibilities."

Deciding to stand her ground, Gaby added, "It would certainly tarnish the land trust's image not to offer residents the opportunity to say an informal farewell to its longtime benefactor. I was hoping you would be willing to serve as master of ceremonies at the event. Say a few words about Mr. Pinkham's contributions to the Woodson Falls Land Trust."

"Humph!" Conway grunted, clearly torn between his apparent dislike for Pinkham and the opportunity to be in the spotlight as head of the land trust. "I thought that old meddler was out of the way once and for all," he muttered under his breath.

Gaby stifled her gasp on hearing this, wondering if Conway, who appeared deep in thought, realized he had spoken aloud. "Excuse me?"

"Can't say I'm sorry he's joined the departed," Conway replied, a bit more loudly, still staring at the floor. He turned his head, meeting Gaby's eyes. "I have big plans for the WFLT. Big plans.

Old Win Pinkham did all he could to throw a monkey wrench into my carefully thought-out strategic scheme for the direction the trust should take in the long-term. Went on and on about the fragmentation of habitat, Pinkham did. Never gave a thought to the fragmentation created by small-scale conservation efforts. Blocked me at every turn, beginning with his plans for that atrocity of a subdivision, Sunrise Hills."

"Well," Gaby said, standing and more than ready to exit the cramped office space. "I better be on my way. Have some errands…" Her voice trailed off as she turned to leave.

"Sit!" Conway ordered. "I'm not done talking to you."

"What do you want, Mr. Conway?" Gaby answered, staying on her feet.

Softening his voice a bit, he said, "I was wondering about that remainder trust you mentioned. How does that work? And when will the WFLT get the money?"

Slowly taking her seat again, Gaby replied, "The trust—the legal term is charitable remainder trust—was invested in conservative financial instruments with a reliable rate of return that was deposited monthly into Mr. Pinkham's personal checking account.

"While Mr. Pinkham enjoyed a charitable deduction when he created the trust, its long-term goal was to provide a steady income stream for him while he was alive and at the same time preserve principal to the extent permitted by market conditions. Given the recent performance of the market and the nature of the securities in the trust, the funds Mr. Pinkham originally allocated to the charitable remainder trust are pretty much intact. Now that he's died, those funds will be distributed to the charitable entities named in the trust. In this case, the Woodson Falls Land Trust is designated as the sole beneficiary of its remaining funds. As I told you, there's a bit over half a million there."

"And just when will the WFLT receive these funds, which, as the old man well knew, are essential to the continuing operation of the land trust and the future acquisition of properties?"

"The law governing the administration of estates requires expenses related to such costs as the funeral and burial of the decedent and fees related to estate administration, as well as any outstanding claims against estate assets to be paid from estate assets. If there were a shortfall, these expenses would be paid from the charitable trust. As it is, I'm fairly certain there are sufficient assets in the estate to pay legally required costs, in addition to the payment of legacies in accordance with Mr. Pinkham's will. It usually takes at least a year to finalize an estate—maybe a bit longer since Mr. Pinkham's estate is complicated by the need to market and sell the subdivision lots—so the land trust can expect to receive the funds left in the charitable trust in a couple of years."

"That long, humph?" Conway sighed, then asked, "Are you certain you don't want to forgo the subdivision headache and just donate that property to us outright?"

"Yes, I'm sure," Gaby replied. "As I explained before, my duty flows to the beneficiaries named in Mr. Pinkham's will."

"Just one more question," Conway ventured. "Would our organization receive the funds from this charitable trust in the event the WFLT merges with other small land trusts in the area?"

"Most likely, yes. The goal is to distribute the charitable trust assets as originally intended by the maker of the trust. Since it's clear that Mr. Pinkham's purpose in creating the trust was ultimately to support land preservation, the funds could make their way to a merged organization if that occurred."

"So, all in good time, and I can move forward on plans for a merger now that a major obstacle has been cleared," Conway said, mostly to himself.

"If you have no further questions, Mr. Conway, I best be going," Gaby said, standing up and walking to the door. "You have a good day."

Gaby stood for a moment once she was out the door. She felt the need to shed the anxiety she'd felt while confined in the small space with a passive-aggressive Conway. *Did Conway imply that he had eliminated Pinkham as a block to his aspirations, or did she misinterpret his statements? Was the man capable of murder?* Gaby was convinced he just might be.

Leaving the land trust office building, Gaby made her way to her Subaru and headed north toward Pine Hill Road. She wanted to call Matt as soon as she got home to convey what she'd just experienced. As she drove through town, she noticed the trooper's cruiser parked outside his office and decided to drop in. Peeking around his office door, she spotted Matt engrossed in paperwork and knocked softly.

"Hey, Gaby! I was going to call you. Got news from Detective Irving."

"Oh? I have news too. Well, not exactly news, just bits and pieces of information," she said, taking the seat across from his desk, which was piled high with papers. "What did you learn?"

"Irving checked out the alibis of each of Pinkham's beneficiaries, as you suggested. Nothing popped. I thought for sure either Samuelson or Wiseman—or both of them—might be involved in some way. Bud Wiseman's alibi was confirmed. He was on a camping trip with friends for the entire Fourth of July weekend. All the way across the state at Pachaug State Forest near the Rhode Island border. Adam Samuelson had originally planned to join Bud on the trip but claimed he hadn't felt well and stayed home at their apartment, but there's no one to verify that."

"So Adam is still in play but not Bud," Gaby mused. "And of course, Conway. I just came from the land trust office. Had a long talk with the secretary, Hilda Morrow, who echoed Win's sense that Conway wanted to capture as many of Woodson Falls' remaining open acres in order to reign as the head of a collection of merged trusts in this area of Connecticut. I may have underestimated Conway's thirst for power. Perhaps he saw Win as standing in the way of his achieving a full-time position with a larger land trust.

"I ran into Conway—literally—when I was leaving the land trust office. He's one scary dude, and he matches the description the New York person gave as well as your own observations of the man. He's a head shorter than I am, tan, balding, well built."

"What made you think he was scary?" Matt asked.

"He muttered something about Mr. Pinkham having been 'taken care of,' but his comments fell short of being a clear admission of guilt. Conway gave me the impression he saw Win as a major block to his ambition to head a larger land trust if he could pull off the merger.

"You said once that people have strange reasons for wanting someone dead. Conway's obsession with heading a merged land trust just might have been a strong enough motive to go after Win. Based on what you learned in checking his background, there's a fair possibility he had the knowledge necessary to create the explosion. And he looks, to me at least, as if he has the physical strength to cause the wound the medical examiner discovered during the autopsy."

"Detective Irving asked me to follow up with Conway based on the New York visitor's report of someone arriving at Pinkham's home as his guests were leaving. I planned to head over there soon," Matt added, standing and buckling on his paraphernalia. "Want to join me?"

"I would," Gaby answered, "but won't that seem odd to Conway?"

"So what?"

Chapter 33

GABY AND MATT walked to the land trust office, which was only a short distance from the town center.

"I'm serious," Gaby said, looking toward Matt. "What will you say if Conway asks what I'm doing there?"

"I'll figure it out. No worries."

Arriving at the land trust office, Matt knocked, then entered unannounced.

"Officer! Can I help you?" Conway asked, standing and moving to shake Matt's hand. Spotting Gaby just behind the trooper, Conway added, "What's *she* doing here?"

"Not your concern," Matt responded, taking out a notepad and pencil. "I'm assisting the state police in the investigation of Winston Pinkham's murder, and I have a few questions."

Conway backed away. "Am I a suspect?"

"If you'll just answer my questions, sir, I'll be out of your hair shortly."

"Okay," Conway said in a subdued voice, taking a seat. Matt moved closer to the man but remained standing, towering over the seated Conway. Gaby hung back, avoiding Conway's eyes as they ranged between her and the trooper.

"In the course of our investigation of Pinkham's murder, we spoke with an individual who reported seeing someone fitting your description arriving at Pinkham's home at 2 Sunrise Trail on July 2, the day of his murder. The description given to the investigating detective by this individual matched my recollection of you after we met the other day."

"Who gave you this information?" Conway asked.

"I'm not at liberty to say," Matt responded. "Did you visit Pinkham that day?"

"Yes, I did," Conway answered defensively. "What of it?"

"Sir, could you tell me when you were there?"

"Well, it was before lunch, I recall," Conway sputtered. "Close to eleven in the morning, if I remember correctly."

"And the purpose of your visit?"

"I went to see Win Pinkham in my role as executive director and chief operating officer of the Woodson Falls Land Trust," Conway announced, needlessly including his titles. "Win had checkbooks belonging to the land trust in his possession. I was there to pick up some checks to cover land trust expenses. It was common knowledge that the man never left his home, requiring anyone doing business with him to come to him."

Conway softened his tone, adding, "I also wanted to offer my assistance with the paperwork that became his responsibility when our treasurer resigned."

A little late for that, Gaby thought, reflecting on the hours she'd spent dealing with Win's tangled financial records along with those of the land trust.

"Hmm…" Matt jotted something in his notebook. "And how long were you there?"

"A half hour, forty-five minutes tops. Win was obviously fatigued, which is why I kept my visit short."

"And he was alive when you left?"

"Of course!" Conway declared. "He seemed tired, as I said. Looked like he was about to doze off. But very much alive."

"And where did you go after leaving Sunrise Trail?"

"Home. Stayed in the rest of the afternoon and evening."

"Can anyone verify that?"

"No. I live alone. I didn't make or receive any phone calls. I did some light exercise, watched the news, made something to eat, and went to bed early."

"Hmm…" Matt closed his notebook. "Anything to add?"

"No, sir."

"Well, thank you for answering my questions," Matt said, extending his hand to shake Conway's and turning to leave.

"Officer? One more thing," Conway said, standing to follow Matt and Gaby to the door.

"When I was leaving Pinkham's house, I noticed a UPS truck out front. It was parked on the side of the road with the driver just sitting in it. It seemed odd to me."

Leaving the land trust office, Matt and Gaby headed back to town.

"What did you think of that?" Gaby asked.

"He's still a suspect in my book. He was seen carrying a briefcase when he went to see Pinkham. We don't know how big it was, but it might have held the weapon used to kill Pinkham as well as some sort of poncho or other covering to protect him from blood spray. We know he has the minimal knowledge necessary to trigger the explosion. Despite his use of Pinkham's nickname and his efforts to conceal his anger toward the man, I still picked up a thread of hostility, although that impression may be colored by your report of your interaction with the man. He seemed 'squirrelly' to me, and he doesn't have an alibi."

"What about that last-minute mention of the UPS truck?"

"Either he made it up to throw us off his trail, or he actually saw the truck. Since Pinkham was known to stay in his house, he would have had to order things to be delivered beyond the food his housekeeper brought. My bet is it's fiction, a feeble attempt to throw suspicion elsewhere."

"Hmm… Didn't you learn Bud was a UPS driver? " Gaby mused. "Or was it Adam?"

"It was Adam. Good thought. Easy enough to check with UPS to see if deliveries were made to Pinkham that day."

"Or verify that Adam was on holiday duty. But didn't Irving say he told him he was home sick?"

"He did, but I can check that as well. What are your thoughts about Adam Samuelson?" Matt asked. "Even though Conway is the more likely suspect, we still would need to rule out any involvement either Samuelson or Wiseman had in all of this, though Wiseman's alibi apparently checked out."

"It's hard to say. You learned Adam was a volunteer with the Prescott Fire Department, which might have given him all the information he needed to set off the explosion. I was pretty shaken up that night, as I mentioned before, but I thought I saw him working with the Prescott firemen at Sunrise Trail the night of the explosion. But if he was home sick, would he have still responded?"

"Returning to the scene of the crime?" Matt speculated. "It often happens with arsonists. They want to see the fruits of their labor."

"I've heard that. A bit ghoulish if you ask me," Gaby responded. "Anyway, I do know that Adam and Bud were after Win to change his will to leave them the two lots they wanted outright. He didn't, though the twenty-percent discount off the asking prices remains in the will. The two of them—Adam and Bud—struck me as pretty manipulative. They may have convinced themselves that they had succeeded in having Win change his will or execute a codicil to that effect."

"Did you say at one point that you wondered whether they had the funds to go through with the purchase?"

"Yes, which would offer a possible motive for killing Win. That is, if they believed he had changed his will to leave the lots to them at no charge. But the why of that is unknown at this point."

The pair parted when they reached Gaby's parked car.

"Let me know if Detective Irving can use anything from your interview with Conway," Gaby said.

"Sure thing," Matt responded. "He may want to talk with you to clarify Conway's statements to you and his power-grab that might serve as a motive."

"No problem," Gaby said, getting into her car. "Good luck with all that paperwork on your desk."

"And good luck with all of yours," Matt smiled, saluting her as he turned into his office.

Chapter 34

GABY WAS WRAPPING UP before the long Labor Day weekend. She had invited Matt for dinner, knowing he'd be on duty for the holiday. She wanted to shower and change into jeans and a fresh shirt before he arrived at five.

Kat barked when the doorbell rang and jumped around Matt as soon as Gaby opened the door. The trooper gave the dog a pat to acknowledge her greeting and handed Gaby a chilled bottle of prosecco, wet with condensation.

"Just had a call from Detective Irving," he announced.

"Oh?"

"They applied for a search warrant of Conway's premises based on our information. Called us 'the dynamic duo,'" Matt said with a smile, moving into the kitchen to open the bubbly while Gaby pulled down two glasses.

"I have some cheese and crackers to go with that," she said, getting out the prepared platter of cheese and fruit and placing it on a tray along with small plates, cocktail napkins, and a basket of crackers. "Inside or out?"

"It's a lovely evening. Let's have this on the patio out front," Matt said, leading the way with the filled glasses. He managed to open the door without spilling a drop. Kat followed Gaby out, with Matt bringing up the rear.

When they were settled and had clinked glasses, Gaby said, "So did a judge issue the search warrant?"

"No, though I was looking forward to being involved in the search of Conway's home," Matt said, smearing a cracker with chèvre cheese and offering it to Gaby, then making another for himself. "The state police usually include the local authorities on a search like this, assuming I would be acquainted with Conway and control the situation better than a stranger might."

Matt took a sip of prosecco and continued. "Irving tried to secure the search warrant based on Conway's visit to Pinkham the day of the murder, his lack of an alibi for the rest of the day and evening, as well as your account regarding Conway's comments when you were with him. I was surprised at that last. Isn't that hearsay?"

"Actually, what he said could be construed to fit one of the few exceptions to the hearsay rule, although it would be a reach. His comments about getting Pinkham 'out of the way' might be considered a 'statement against penal interest,' meaning that it sounds like a confession. But without a lot more to go on, I'm not surprised a judge declined to issue a search warrant."

"Irving thought that Major Crimes' diligence in ruling out any other suspects might help, but it didn't."

"What did Irving hope to find in a search?"

"Possible weapon as well as any blood-stained garments," Matt replied. "He did secure Conway's permission to search the land trust office and the shed abutting the land trust building they use to store equipment. Conway went with the detectives to unlock the office. The search there came up empty.

"There were a number of machetes hanging in the shed. Conway said volunteers were free to use them when they worked on land trust trails. Apparently, the shed is left unlocked so volunteers can access the equipment when they're free to work."

"That opens a can of worms! Pretty much anybody could be involved," Gaby commented. "Did they find anything that could be considered evidence?"

Matt took another sip of prosecco, then continued. "One of the detectives involved in the search took each of them down from their hooks to examine. One appeared to have dried blood between the handle and the blade. Conway stated someone could have nicked himself in the process of using or cleaning the machete. It was taken as evidence to be tested in the lab for blood type and fingerprints."

"Don't keep me in suspense! Did the lab find anything?"

"There was enough blood to match it to Pinkham's. His was A negative. Type A negative blood is fairly rare, making it unlikely to have come from a volunteer, although we'd have to get blood types from all of them to be sure. Regardless, the presence of A negative blood strongly supported the theory that the machete was used to kill Pinkham. The lab should be able to confirm that it's his. The medical examiner said the machete blade could have made the nick in Pinkham's vertebrae. As you might expect, there were lots of fingerprints on the handle, including Conway's, but there was no way to know when the machete was used."

"That's something to work with, at least," Gaby said, getting up to take the tray back inside. "Did you ever follow up on Conway's claim that a UPS truck was parked outside Win's house the day of the murder?"

"Yes. While they do deliver on Sundays, there was nothing scheduled for delivery to Pinkham on the second. Samuelson wasn't scheduled to work that day either. Which makes Conway's claim of having seen the truck more and more suspect."

"Interesting," Gaby said, then added, "I figured you'll have to be up bright and early tomorrow morning, so I planned an early dinner. How are you with a grill?"

"My specialty. What are we having?"

"Knowing you're a meat-and-potatoes man, I decided on steak and baked potatoes. I made a tomato salad and took out some homemade rolls I keep in the freezer for such occasions. There's a grill out on the deck. I thought we'd eat there. Red wine okay?"

"Absolutely. I'll heat up the grill after I open the wine," Matt replied, taking the bottle from Gaby.

Gaby headed out to the deck with a basket of rolls and a small tray with butter, sour cream, chives, and steak sauce that she added to the table she'd set in the afternoon. Matt followed with the wine and two glasses while Gaby scooted into the kitchen to retrieve the steaks and salad. The potatoes were baking in the oven, shrouded in aluminum wrap. When they were done, she'd have Matt keep them warm them on the grill.

"I wonder if we'll ever learn who killed Win. I hope the case will be solved eventually instead of just becoming another cold case," Gaby mused after she and Matt had taken a sip of wine and he'd laid the steaks on the grill.

Kat had planted herself next to the trooper, her tail wagging away. "I think Kat's in love with you," she said with a fond smile aimed at her pet.

"Hmm…" Matt reached down to scratch Kat's head. "She has excellent taste in men."

Gaby laughed.

"I'm still inclined to suspect Conway," she said. "His drive to become the full-time executive director of a merged land trust put him in conflict with Win, especially when he recognized how much power Win had to rouse people to block his plan. Apparently, Win was quite vociferous in his objections, reaching out to key members to voice his concerns. As a longtime devotee of the land trust and a former president of the group, his status was likely to persuade members to oppose Conway's plans. Feels like a motive to me, but then I don't have to try the case." She moved to the table. "Let's eat."

After they'd finished dinner, Gaby offered Matt dessert. "Homemade apple pie?"

"Ice cream with that?"

"Of course. Will vanilla do?"

Chapter 35

It was sunny, with only a gentle breeze on the mid-September Saturday of the land trust picnic in Winston Pinkham's memory. The sky was so clear you could see all the way to Massachusetts. Volunteers had hauled hay bales to the hilltop site for people to sit on. They brought grills as well, which had been fired up to cook the burgers and franks and keep the large pot of baked beans piping hot. A long table set up under a tent held starters, salads and desserts donated by volunteers along with plastic cutlery, paper plates and napkins. Another table held urns of iced tea and lemonade and a stack of disposable cups.

The land trust had sent a special invitation to its members announcing the memorial picnic and advertised the affair in the local paper. Word-of-mouth also served to attract a large crowd to the event.

Gaby and Hilda had planned a brief program celebrating Pinkham's work with the land trust over the past fifty years. Val Conway had been coaxed into the role of master of ceremonies, but the program featured Ed Holloway, a past president of the trust and longtime friend of Pinkham's, charged with recapping Winston Pinkham's contributions to and involvement with the organization. Following his speech, Hilda would explain the plan to plant the seed papers with written memories and tributes to the trust's departed benefactor, then invite everyone to pen a message on the seed paper laid out on another table after they had eaten.

While Gaby had assisted with planning the picnic and had arranged for the purchase and delivery of boxes and boxes of hamburgers, hot dogs and buns, she had declined to take a visible role in the affair. She would enjoy the picnic with Matt and write her own tribute to her dear friend when the time came.

Gaby mingled with the crowd. Many of her acquaintances stopped to express their condolences, knowing she had been close to the old man. As people began to settle with their meals, Gaby took a seat on a large hay bale and waited for Matt to join her. She was glad he had taken the day off. He had told her he expected the event to be upsetting for her and wanted to provide his support.

Bud Wiseman and Adam Samuelson were deep in conversation as they walked toward her carrying plates full of food, looking for an empty hay bale to sit on in one of the circles. Gaby quickly turned her head, hoping they wouldn't notice her. She was surprised they had attended the memorial picnic, then realized they probably were taking advantage of the free meal.

The pair continued their conversation as they took a seat behind her, facing in the opposite direction. Despite the rumble of the crowd, she could clearly hear what they were saying.

Bud growled, "That damn judge, yelling at us for being late to Pinky's hearing and then refusing to even look at the letter we brought. And we worked so hard to get it just right. Prove Pinky wanted us to have the lots free-and-clear if he died."

"And that damn lawyer sending us up there," Adam responded, "all sweet and helpful. Probably knew the judge would blow up at us."

"It's just wrong, after all the time and trouble…" Bud's remaining words were lost as he gobbled down a hot dog.

Gaby spotted Matt as he headed toward her with two plates. One held a hot dog and some salad, the other heaped with a burger, potato salad and baked beans. He was dressed in a short-sleeved, blue-striped shirt that accentuated his muscular arms, the radio dangling from his belt the only indication he was a trooper. She held her finger to her lips to signal him not to greet her, tossing her head in the direction of the two men seated behind her. Matt followed her lead, a puzzled look in his eyes as he handed Gaby a plate and sat beside her.

"You never met them, but Adam and Bud are right behind us," she whispered. "They seem to be talking about those lots in the Sunrise Hills subdivision they've been focused on."

Matt nodded that he understood, smiling his greeting to her.

"…still can't believe you did that!" Bud was saying. "Pinky was our friend! How could you?"

"We needed those lots to pay off our gambling debts. And he was taking too long to die!"

"But still! Killing him? That's no solution," Bud argued.

"Aren't you being ungrateful," Adam mumbled. "After all the trouble I went to get the UPS truck I used on Saturday."

"I still don't understand how."

"Pocketed the keys when I turned in my run sheet. Boss was so eager to leave for the holiday, he never even noticed."

Bud mumbled something unintelligible, followed by a louder complaint. "I took the machete from the shed because I thought you were going to be doing something on the trails, not so you could…" He lowered his voice. "…kill that old man. There's no way anyone would know it was you, is there?"

"Don't think so," Adam chimed in. "I pulled off the perfect crime for the two of us, but it didn't do us any good. Wish you hadn't admitted I wasn't on the camping trip with you and the guys, though."

"I told you before, I'm sorry about that. Barry kept going on and on about how sad it was you couldn't be there. I didn't see any reason not to tell that detective who called that you stayed home because you felt sick. But so what? No one checked on you, did they?"

"Nah."

The men were silent for a while, then Adam said, "We still get the twenty-percent discount on the lots. Maybe we can scrape together the money to buy at least one of them when the road goes in."

"I've heard enough," Matt murmured to Gaby, setting his half-eaten meal aside on the grass and getting up. Moving around the hay bales to stand in front of Samuelson and Wiseman, he stuck his hand out in greeting and said, "Hey, you two new in town? Haven't seen you around Woodson Falls before."

Adam and Bud both stood to shorten the distance between them and the tall trooper. Adam shook Matt's hand and said, "Adam Samuelson. I used to volunteer for the land trust. Me and my friend here, Bud Wiseman, helped Mr. Pinkham with the subdivision he was planning. And you?"

"Matthew Thomas, the resident state trooper for Woodson Falls, and you fellows, are under arrest for the murder of Winston Pinkham, conspiracy to commit murder, and arson.

"Please turn around." Taking out a pair of plastic zip ties, he quickly handcuffed each man, joining them with yet another tie while he recited the standard Miranda warning. "Have anything to say at this time?" Both men shook their heads. The startled crowd just stared as the trooper patted both men down before leading them away to his cruiser.

Gaby trailed behind, though she knew she couldn't follow Matt to wherever he was taking the pair.

Matt called the next morning. "So sorry I couldn't be there for you for the rest of the day. And that I wasn't able to call earlier. It was a long day and night."

"I understand, of course. What happened after you left with Adam and Bud?"

"I brought the pair to Prescott where they were booked. We offered them attorneys, but Samuelson said he'd had enough of lawyers after meeting you." Matt chuckled. "We stuck them in separate interrogation rooms after they were booked. Wiseman broke after a couple of hours and told us the whole thing. Samuelson broke a few hours later. It being the weekend, they won't be arraigned until Monday. They'll be kept in the holding cells at the Prescott Police Department until then."

Epilogue

GABY DECIDED to take a break from her work to swim with Kat out to Hemlock Island, the smallest of the three uninhabited islands in the middle of Woodson Lake. Even now, in early October, the late morning sun had managed to push the air temperature to a bit over seventy. The waters of the lake, still warm from the summer heat, were comfortable for swimming. The shade of the island's many hemlocks left a narrow band of sunlit beach offering a bit of warmth once the pair emerged from the water. It promised to be another beautiful early fall day in Woodson Falls.

Gaby reflected on all that had transpired since the memorial picnic celebrating Winston Pinkham's life and the arrest of Adam Samuelson and Bud Wiseman. Plea bargain arrangements for both Samuelson and Wiseman served to avoid a lengthy trial.

Given Samuelson's direct involvement in both the murder of Pinkham and the explosion on Sunrise Trail, he had been sentenced to life with the possibility of parole. Wiseman was sentenced to a lengthy parole for his part in aiding Samuelson.

Pinkham's cremains had finally been released by the medical examiner's office and buried in the Vermont family plot. Gaby had made progress in administering his estate. The road and drainage system for the Sunrise Hills subdivision had been initiated and the lots appraised. The site of Pinkham's destroyed house at 2 Sunrise Trail was no longer fenced in and garlanded with crime tape. The property and the subdivision lots were being marketed by Robin Meyerson, the real estate agent Gaby had retained for this purpose. Pinkham's bank accounts had been transferred to a single account in the name of the estate and his investment accounts retitled as estate accounts.

Gaby's thoughts turned back to the early morning call she'd gotten from Sylvia Grant that had prompted her to take this swim. Her friend and colleague at Columbia University, Sylvia had told Gaby about the sudden death of their friend and fellow philosophy professor, Ellen DelMonaco. She was killed instantly, hit by a driver who had run a red light.

Ellen had been more than a colleague to Gaby. She had served as chair of Gaby's dissertation committee, guiding her thoughtfully through the rigorous process of developing a research project and working through to the results. Ellen had challenged Gaby's thinking and fine-tuned her writing, ensuring that the final product would be one they'd both be proud of. Gaby had adopted Ellen's approach as her own in working with doctoral students who had reached this final, critical phase of their education. The quality of their dissertation research would, in large measure, determine their success in whatever professional path they chose to follow.

Gaby enjoyed working with doctoral students. They challenged her intellectually, as well as offering the satisfaction of watching a person blossom under her guidance. That was, if they were as diligent in their work as she was in guiding them—sometimes a big "if."

It was an issue Gaby often had discussed with Sylvia and Ellen. The problem was particularly acute with students whose major course of study was in another department. University policy required doctoral students to select a dissertation committee of between two and three faculty members, with at least one committee member from a department different from the one in which the student was registered.

Most students chose as a second committee member someone from a discipline that supported the student's proposed study. And a few hunted down a professor they'd heard was supportive, even though they had never taken a course in the professor's discipline. It was as if the candidate expected that faculty member to give them a private tutorial on the relevant aspects of the supporting discipline!

Gaby recalled one candidate whose study involved the ethics of business finance. He had sought Gaby as a member of his committee because of her expertise in the study of ethics, yet this student had never taken a course in the subject. He also proved resistant to any guidance and seldom consulted with her on the progress of the study, despite her many attempts to connect with him.

After the student handed her what he assumed was a completed project, she ended up refusing to approve the dissertation and allow the student to proceed to the oral defense that would mark the end of the process. It was a rare move, and one she didn't make lightly. She first consulted with the business school faculty member serving as the committee chair, who admitted having had little input into the study.

Gaby had suggested that the student reengage in the research using a specific ethical framework to better focus the work. The committee chair concurred. This meant, essentially, that the student had to begin the process all over again. She never saw the student after that, nor had she expected to. *What was his name?*

She searched her memory as she swam back to the lakeshore, emerging from the water with a gasp. Grabbing her towel to dry off quickly and give Kat a rub down, Gaby raced to her car where she had left her cell phone. She had to call Matt.

Her meandering memories of working with Ellen had finally dredged up the recollection of that one troublesome student. And his name was Gunther Grossmann!

Thank you for reading *Woodson Falls: 2 Sunset Trail*
If you've enjoyed reading this book, please leave a review on your favorite review site. It helps me reach more readers who may enjoy visiting Woodson Falls.

Subscribe to my newsletter at
emeraldlakebooks.com/gabyquinn
to be notified when the next book in
the Gaby Quinn Mystery series is released.

Author's Note

STEPHEN KING ADVISES WRITERS to "kill their darlings," referring to those characters the writer has come to know and care about, and I followed King's recommendation in this third book in the Gaby Quinn Mystery series.

Woodson Falls: 2 Sunrise Trail is a work of fiction. As a character, Winston Pinkham is an amalgam of several of my elder law clients and my father. Pinkham appeared in the first title in the series, *Woodson Falls: 16 Lakeview Terrace*, mostly to reveal something of protagonist Gabriella Quinn's personality and her approach to legal clients, especially the elderly, through her interactions with him. Pinkham had a more prominent role in a secondary plot line in *Woodson Falls: 9 Donovan's Way*, in relation to his planned subdivision, Sunrise Hills. He is the unfortunate victim in this third book, and I must say I'm sad to see him go.

When I sit down to write a new adventure for Gaby, I've already made some notes about what I want to be sure to include, checking these off in a spiral notebook as I address them. I tend to visualize scenes before writing them and know I'm on the right track when my characters begin to talk to me, nudging me in the direction the writing should take. Although I don't formally plot each scene, I usually have a good idea of where the story is headed. Not so with *2 Sunrise Trail*.

9 Donovan's Way ended with a cliffhanger when Gaby received a warning from a stranger referring to her late husband, Joe. While I had a vague notion of what the underlying issue was—why Gaby and Joe were attacked on the streets of New York, an attack that killed Joe and scarred Gaby—it ended up being unrealistic and had to be rejected. In this current mystery, I introduced the possibility that the attack was aimed at Gaby. The conundrum these dueling motives created made the writing more difficult.

Unlike the first two books in the series, *2 Sunrise Trail* drew more from my experience as the chief elected official of a small Connecticut town than from my practice as an elder law and estate planning attorney. Managing the day-to-day operations of a small town forces the town's leader to become familiar with both the law and politics related to a host of issues—in this story, a bit about the law and politics surrounding land use and preservation.

All authors rely, to some extent, on expert input into a story line. I am immensely grateful to Sherman's Fire Marshal, Dave Lathrop, who provided the key information allowing Pinkham's murderer to escape the devastating explosion of Pinkham's home meant to mask evidence of his murder. I continue to grow as a fiction writer as I work with Tara R. Alemany, owner and founder of Emerald Lake Books, as well as her partner, Mark Gerber. Their comments on the manuscript are key to sharpening the story line as well as the writing.

I enjoy coming up with foods that Gaby orders or makes. If you're interested, you can find the recipe for the chicken salad special she orders at the café on my website at woodsonfalls.com/chickensalad and the tomato salad she prepares for a dinner with Matt Thomas at woodsonfalls.com/obesetomatoes.

If you've enjoyed returning to Woodson Falls in this latest mystery, I'm hoping you'll return to learn what becomes of the new bookstore in town and who might be the next victim in this small rural town in the upcoming *Woodson Falls: 3 Shadow Lane.*

— Andrea

About the Author

HAVING RECEIVED A LIBRARY CARD before she began kindergarten (requiring her cursive signature), Andrea began her writing career at the age of five with a short story describing the seasons. Her next endeavor, at the age of nine, was a novella featuring Christine O'Leary. So began Andrea's long love affair with the written word.

Singularly focused on a nursing career, Andrea continued to write for pleasure throughout high school and college. After earning a master's degree to teach nursing, she was offered a position as a nurse editor with a major nursing publisher, where she honed her writing skills through editing others' works.

Intrigued by the intersection of medical ethics and the law, Andrea attended law school and, upon her admission to the Connecticut and New York bars, established a solo practice in estate planning, probate and elder law.

Andrea had long considered writing a mystery series based on some of her legal cases. The opportunity to do so came when her husband John's Parkinson's disease progressed to the point where he was unable to engage in his usual active lifestyle. They began their collaboration on the first book in the Gaby Quinn Mystery series, *Woodson Falls: 16 Lakeview Terrace*, in response to John's longing to do something.

After leaving a long career in a "publish or perish" university setting, it was hard for Andrea not to view writing fiction as lying on paper. John helped her to push the uneasy feeling that was the seed for that first book into a believable plotline. It was Andrea's long service as the chief elected official of a small town in Connecticut that provided the story's sense of place.

Having caught the mystery bug, Andrea has continued the series with *Woodson Falls: 9 Donovan's Way* and *Woodson Falls: 2 Sunrise Trail*. She has already embarked on a planned fourth book in the series and knows that her twenty-five years as a practicing attorney offers fodder for many other stories to explore.

Andrea is the author of three award-winning texts in the area of nursing education and staff development, as well as numerous articles in peer-reviewed nursing and education journals. She collects teddy bears and birdhouses, loves to garden and bake bread, and writes from Sherman, Connecticut.

To explore her books and learn more about Andrea's writing process as well as the backgrounds of people and places in Woodson Falls, visit woodsonfalls.com.

If you're interested in having Andrea come speak to your group or organization about this book, the Gaby Quinn Mystery series, or about the writing process, either online or in person, you can contact her at emeraldlakebooks.com/oconnor.

For more great books, please visit us at
emeraldlakebooks.com.

EMERALD LAKE
BOOKS
Sherman, Connecticut

www.ingramcontent.com/pod-product-compliance
Lightning Source LLC
Chambersburg PA
CBHW050849190726
48286CB00007B/2289